# *Ride*
# *On*
# *Rapunzel*

## Fairytales for Feminists

Attic Press
Dublin

First Published in Ireland in 1992 by
Attic Press
4 Upper Mount Street
Dublin 2

British Library Cataloguing in Publication Data

Binchy, Maeve
Ride On Rapunzel: (Fairytales for Feminists Series)
I. Title II. Series
823.01089287 [FS]
ISBN 1-85594-051-5

Cinderella Re-examined, Rapunzel's Revenge, Goldilocks Finds a Home, The Princesses' Forum, Hi Ho, It's Off to Strike We Go! Jack's Mother and The Beanstalk first appeared in *Rapunzel's Revenge* (Attic Press, 1985). Snida, The Frog Prince Revisited, That'll Teach Her first appeared in *Ms Muffet and Others* (Attic Press, 1986). The Fate of Aoife and the Children of Aobh, Some Day My Prince Will Come, The Witch-Hunt, The Frog Prince, Thumbelina first appeared in *Mad & Bad Fairies* (Attic Press, 1987). Ms Snow White Wins Case In High Court, The Budgeen, Snow-Fight Defeats Patri-Arky, The Twelve Dancing Princesses first appeared in *Sweeping Beauties* (Attic Press, 1989). Riding Hood, The King, The Queen and The Donkey Man, Happy Ever After and Other Obsessions first appeared in Cinderella on the Ball (Attic Press, 1991).

Cover Design: Kate White
Illustrations: Siobhán Condon, Denise Kierans, Barbara Nolan, Paula Nolan, Catherine McConville & Kate White
Origination: Attic Press
Printing: Guernsey Press Co. Ltd

# Contents

# Cinderella Re-examined

ONCE UPON A time there were three sisters whose appearance is immaterial but the eldest girl Thunder had a ferocious temper, and a great greed for money. She was constantly scanning the papers and magazines to find out where she might be likely to meet wealthy men. 'Don't love for money,' she warned the others. 'But love where money is.'

The second sister was called Lightning, and she wasn't as obsessed with wealth as Thunder was, but she had plenty to keep her busy. Lightning had this very firm belief that you never got a husband, wealthy or impoverished, unless you played the game by the rules, and the rules were to promise everything and deliver nothing. Lightning had been called some very unattractive names in her time, but she just laughed because she said those kind of men weren't husband material anyway.

Thunder and Lightning had a younger sister who was called Cinderella. She didn't have any firm philosophy like they did, so they thought she was a bit dull. Cinderella ran the house for the family without much complaint, so Thunder and Lightning thought she was a bit wet as well. But Cinderella shrugged and said what the hell. Father had given Thunder the money to open a boutique and he had given Lightning the money to set up a beauty shop, and he wouldn't hear of giving Cinderella the money to buy the franchise for a fast food chain which is what she wanted, so she might as well make the best of it until she had enough money of her own one day. She seemed to enjoy going to the market and buying food in bulk and she was always cheerful. She was doing two correspondence courses as well as a degree from the Open University, and she never crossed the paths of Thunder and Lightning, and Father was pleased to have nice meals put in front of him, so everyone in the household seemed reasonably content.

From time to time, like most families, they had disappointments. Cinderella would ask her father to buy her even a small fish-and-chip shop, but to no avail. Thunder might go on the prowl, certain she had found wealthy men, only to discover that they were penniless fortune hunters. Very often Lightning's date of the evening drove away in a terrible rage. But nothing more serious than that disturbed their peaceful ways.

Then one day all hell broke loose. It was the day when they announced that the king was going to give a huge ball at the palace and his handsome playboy son, who had broken many hearts but without managing to make any commitments whatsoever, was going to be there and the gossip columns all said that the prince was going to make a determined effort to find a wife at last, having tried everything else that the world could offer; there were few areas of mystery left to him and he was going to begin the long and responsible process of settling down. Thunder was in a frenzy of excitement. When she had hoped to marry wealth she had never dared to set her sights as high as the prince, but after all why not? She was a highly fashionable woman. She settled like a storm cloud in her boutique and organised it so that those of her customers who might be her rivals got hideous clothes while her outfit was a dazzler. Lightning felt that she had the whole thing sewn up. What these foolish hussies had done wrong was to give all to the prince when he looked like needing it. Lightning was going to tempt the prince out of his poor simple basic mind. She hired a plastic surgeon for her beauty salon in order to make her own bosom more curvaceous than ever. At the same time the plastic surgeon was to disimprove any clients that might be rivals. Not disfigure them but dull them up a bit. Cinderella wasn't at all interested in the ball. She thought it was mildly interesting in a sociological way, but she hadn't much time to concentrate on it on account of doing several papers which had all come up at once in her correspondence courses, and entering a competition in a magazine. There was some ridiculous Charm Course or something as first prize but there were six runner-up prizes of nice sums of money and since Father still wouldn't agree to listen to her financial proposals, she knew she would have to find the money herself. It seemed a silly sort of competition but still, it was only the cost of a stamp. So Cinderella entered.

Six weeks before the great ball at the palace Cinderella was visited by a most extraordinary woman, in an insane-looking tiara. There was also a photographer who started to take pictures of Cinderella opening the door and the idiotic woman in the net dress and the silly thing on her head started to whimper and cry out that Cinderella had won the Amazing Charm Course worth hundreds and hundreds of pounds. Cinderella discussed it long and earnestly but she met with diamond hard opposition from the magazine columnist who called herself Fairy

Godmother. FG was in fact deeply affronted that Cinderella wanted to sell her Charm Course to the highest bidder. She wouldn't countenance offering Cinderella a cash prize. It was the Charm Course or nothing. Cinderella decided it must be nothing; she had no time to learn how to walk gracefully, how to swing her legs out of a car, or how to eat cake without making crumbs. She was quite happy to put some make-up on her face but she felt her allotted life-span was much too short to waste any of it learning about drawing hollows in her cheeks and how to apply loose powder and then dust most of it off. As politely as she could she thanked FG, the Fairy Godmother, and said she had to go back to her studies.

'You also get an Art Appreciation Course, a Music Course and a Five Easy Steps to Bluffing Your Way in Literature Course,' said the awful FG, 'and lots of books and records and pictures as well.'

Cinderella got out her pocket calculator. She could sell the books, records and pictures. There would be a small profit in it. She would do it.

The household continued reasonably happily, Thunder rolling unmercifully around her boutique, Lightning flashing around her beauty salon and Cinderella yawning her way through *Care of the Cuticles* and what to pack for a weekend house-party.

'Do pay attention, Cinderella,' said the head of the Charm Course. 'You're going to need all this when you go to the ball.'

'Oh no, I haven't any intention of going to the ball,' Cinderella said and she had to sit down suddenly and inelegantly from shock when she realised that part of the prize she had won involved her going to the ball decked in borrowed jewellery and furs, and travelling

Siobhán Condon

in a big sleek car which was hers for the night only. She would be photographed in all her finery and girls everywhere would envy her the wonderful opportunities she had won.

'But it's going to be a very boring evening, and I'll be worried about all this gear that doesn't belong to me,' Cinderella began. Nonsense, they wouldn't listen to her. Everyone in the country was positively aching for such a chance. Cinderella felt depressed when it was put to her that way, but agreed that she had better shut up and go along with it. It would all be over soon and she could sell these immense coffrets of cosmetics and a lot of other over-priced goods that didn't interest her.

Thunder and Lightning were so busy in their own preparations for the ball that it never occurred to them to ask Cinderella if she was going or not, and they were most aggrieved when the big car turned up to collect her. Cinderella offered them a lift. She said, reasonably, that there was room for half the street in it but Lightning and Thunder said of course they weren't going to arrive, three girls together; it would be pathetic. They looked suspiciously at Cinderella's appearance, which seemed to have improved very deceitfully. Her dress and extraordinarily elegant glass shoes took them by surprise.

'It's all part of the prize, remember, the Fairy godmother prize,' Cinderella tried to explain, but Thunder's brow darkened and Lightning's eyes flashed and they went back to their own rooms for final titivation in very bad tempers indeed.

The man from the car firm said the car had to be back by twelve midnight, and the furrier said that he had to have his mink back then too, otherwise it wouldn't be properly insured. The jeweller said he had

10

to put the diamond necklace into the night safe at midnight, and Cinderella said that was all fine, the sooner the better as far as she was concerned.

The palace was big and draughty and even though they had gone to great trouble setting out a banquet, a lot of the food was cold by the time it had made the long journey through the stone corridors. There was a great amount of waste, Cinderella noticed, not to mention thieving. She could see that one of the fellows in a powdered wig, who was meant to be in charge, had a nice little number going for himself with boxes and bags; these were being taken out as if they were rubbish but were in fact full of first rate food waiting to be loaded on to a waiting lorry.

The king was old and had a sad smile. He hoped that everyone was having a good time and that the prince might lay off the booze a bit and try to focus on some of the young women, preferably a young woman with a great deal of money, since the palace was near financial ruin. The reason behind this very extravagant ball was the hope of ensnaring the daughter of a self-made millionaire, who would be so thrilled about the royal connection that every bill would be paid unquestioningly. Wouldn't that be great? The king sighed heavily.

Cinderella was near him as he sighed and she felt sorry for him.

'It must have been a desperate job organising this lot,' she said sympathetically.

'It was,' said the king, 'and it cost a fortune.'

'It could have been a bit better organised,' said Cinderella.

'Well, we spent months organising it,' said the king sadly,' and do you know, I think we're running low on

11

wine, and there must have been thousands of pounds worth of strawberries and they didn't stretch at all.'

'Oh, they stretched all right,' Cinderella said. 'If you asked someone from security to look out in the back yard, you'd see them stretching into refrigerated lorries.'

That was the start of it. The king was delighted with Cinderella. She took him on a tour of his own palace and pointed out how savings could be made.

She explained that the old-fashioned kitchen was losing him more money than he could imagine. She indicated where the freezers should be and how the stores should be kept. She took out her pocket calculator from her small silver handbag and did some sums, because she thought it would be quite possible for the palace to go into the business of serving food to visitors.

The king became very excited. He took off his crown and Cinderella took off the glass slippers that were crucifying her, and together they planned a turn-around in the palace finances. So engrossed did they become that midnight was upon them, and the furriers and jewellers and the car people were hysterical trying to repossess their property. Casually, Cinderella peeled off the diamonds, handed over the car keys and her cloakroom ticket for the mink. She and the king talked on, but in order not to be anti-social they went back to the ballroom. The prince spotted Cinderella towards the end of the ball and asked her to dance.

'Oh, please, please do,' said the king, hoping that by some wild chance his dim son might marry this financial wizard and keep her in the family.

The prince danced well, if drunkenly. Cinderella said it was like walking on knives trying to dance in those shoes, so she took them off again and left them under a table out of the way. Without actually seeing her sisters she could feel the disapproval of Thunder and Lightning, but the prince was so boring that Cinderella excused herself and left the floor. She could only find one of her shoes but decided it was not worth hunting for the other. They were dangerous anyway and she was going to have a word with the manufacturers about them. She said goodbye to the king and hitched a lift home.

The gossip columns were full of the prince's agony. He had met the one true love of his life and all he had to remember her by, and even to identify her by, was a glass slipper. The papers made a real meal out of it.

Cinderella rang him up and asked him to stop being so crass and to examine his assumption that every woman would want to win him just because he was a prince. She said that if he would forgive plain speaking he should watch the gargle as well, and while she was on the phone, could he get his father, there were a few more things she had intended to say to him.

The prince was peeved and even more so when he noticed that Cinderella was soon a regular visitor to the palace, and then an employee, and was then in charge of the entire catering side of things. The prince admitted that the coffee was fresh, good and hot, which it had never been before. The food was excellent, and the palace was open to visitors three afternoons a week, which brought in a great deal of revenue. Cinderella and the king were hatching up more and more ideas. There were plans for a conference centre. The king was going to give a lot of land to the Corpo to make it into a public park, and this meant that the king did not have to pay the gardeners; that the Corpo did,

13

and everyone seemed pleased.

The prince kept the glass slipper in his briefcase along with his vodka and white lemonade. Occasionally he would take it out and stroke the glass and wish he was the kind of man Cinderella would marry.

He was sitting playing with the shoe one day when Cinderella came in.

'I really think you should see someone about this foot fetish you have,' she said to him kindly. 'I'm sure it's something they could cure.'

'Please, please will you marry me?' burst out the prince.

'No, thank you,' said Cinderella courteously. 'I prefer to be free, you see. But I'd like you to think of me as a friend or an adviser.'

'Friend! What kind of friend are you to me? Putting me off the drink, trying to drag me to a shrink, saying I've got a thing about feet. That's not friendship.'

Cinderella gently took the shoe away from the prince and held it up to the light.

'Listen here, prince, why don't you help our group? We're trying to get shoes like this banned, crippling young girls' feet, and lethal too. Suppose somebody kicked you in a glass slipper. It could cut your feet off, just like that.'

The prince looked up with dulled eyes. 'I suppose it's a bit like the Chinese foot binding,' he said.

'Now,' cried Cinderella triumphantly, 'that's better. Come to the protest meeting on Tuesday. Your name on the paper will be a help and it will give you something to do, take you out of the house a bit, bring you out of yourself.'

*Siobhán Condon*

The prince looked happier than he had for weeks. He was not a bad boy but Cinderella thought she had done the right thing in refusing to marry him. A woman had enough to do these days without taking on a husband who had to be given things to do to keep him occupied. Besides, her post as Chief Executive of Palace Enterprises was going to keep her busy and very happy ever after.

*Maeve Binchy*

# Rapunzel's Revenge

RAPUNZEL MURPHY was a woman of no means but much imagination. She had worked in many different jobs but the tide of recession was high and ensured she remained flotsam in the sea of unemployment. She frequently pictured herself, jazz singer extraordinaire in one of Dublin's top music clubs, campaigner for civil rights among the downtrodden masses or helping her friend Pauline Hyland grow her own food, and investigate the healing powers of wild plants on her small holding in west Donegal.

Rapunzel was ruminating in this fashion one Thursday morning, returning from her weekly excursion to the unemployment office, when she was interrupted by a clean-cut, smartly-dressed man in his twenties. Before she could gather her wits she found herself being invited to participate in a marketing exercise for a new Shineon shampoo. She was offered fifty pounds a day. With images of a holiday at Pauline's in Donegal flashing through her mind, she willingly answered the man's questions on her age, family background and next of kin.

He seemed delighted to hear that she was an only child and that her nearest living relative was an aunt who lived in Australia. Commenting on her luxurious head of hair, he told Rapunzel that she was just the sort of 'girl' they were looking for. Would she be free to come to the company office the following day? Would she be free! Her feet could not carry her quickly enough to telephone Pauline to relate the good news.

To Rapunzel's surprise, Pauline was less than enthusiastic.

'Fifty pounds a day for getting your hair washed? Sounds a bit fishy to me. I've a feeling that company has been involved in animal experimentation and chemical pollution of the rivers.'

'Well, I'm sick of being broke for good causes. Fifty quid is fifty quid and it will mean that we can have a good weekend together down at your place.'

The next morning as the warm water trickled down the back of her neck Rapunzel felt distinctly uncomfortable. She was sitting in the plush 'product testing salon', having her hair shampooed with 'New Improved Shineon'. Rory Prince, marketing manager, who had greeted her that morning as she signed the consent forms, was everything that she despised, sleek and well-groomed, every inch the image maker.

'Every man will fall at your feet, my dear,' he said condescendingly, 'after you have used Shineon.'

'Spare me this,' thought Rapunzel. 'The things I do for money!'

Sitting under the hair dryer Rapunzel felt a strange, tingling sensation all over her scalp. She hoped that she was not going to be allergic to this stuff. They had assured her that it was absolutely non-allergenic, but she did not trust that Rory Prince one bit.

After the third wash and blow dry she definitely felt peculiar. She had the sensation that she had more hair than she had started out with that morning. There were no mirrors in the 'salon' so she could not immediately check this out. Lunch was provided for her, and very nice it was too, but she got a few strange looks in the company canteen. When her hair fell into her soup for the fourth time she really began to get suspicious.

By four o'clock in the afternoon a controlled panic had broken out in the salon. White-coated lab technicians scurried about with bottles of strange-smelling solution and whispered together in corners. Even the smooth mask of Rory Prince's face could not disguise his disquiet.

'Well, well, dear, this is proving to be a most interesting experiment indeed. We would like you to be our guest for the night so that we can monitor the results. We have a charming suite of rooms upstairs which you may use.'

'I'm sorry, but I can't possibly stay,' said Rapunzel. 'I've got a weight-lifting class tonight ...'

Rory Prince curled his lip in distaste, before the suave veneer descended again. 'Well, I'm sorry too, my dear,' he said, 'but you should have read the small print in your contract. It states that you must stay until we consider that the tests are complete. Let's not have any unpleasantness, my dear.' He propelled her in the direction of the lift.

Despite the soft bed and the luxurious surroundings of the suite, Rapunzel realised that she was a prisoner. There was no telephone in the room, no writing materials and Prince had locked the door behind him as he left. Tossing and turning on the bed with great difficulty, since her hair was now down to her knees, Rapunzel wished she had listened to Pauline's doubts.

'I might have known that any company that polluted rivers, and didn't care about bunny rabbits, wouldn't care about people either.'

At the organic smallholders' group Pauline made enquiries about Shineon Beauty Products and heard a rumour that they had closed a factory some years before when they were threatened with a public enquiry over serious environmental pollution. It was said, too, that they had strange links with a covert mercenary organisation in central Africa! Pauline grew uneasy when Rapunzel failed to arrive on Friday night as planned. By the next evening she had become alarmed. Rapunzel might be weight training, but she was no heavyweight when it came to dealing with multinational corporations. Still, it was a bit rich of her not to make contact. On Tuesday morning Pauline boarded the bus, trying to suppress her rising anger and anxiety.

Rapunzel clambered around the growing mass of tangled hair. By this stage (had she really been here five days?) she sat five feet off the ground in one corner of the room, singing quietly to herself. Dozens of black plastic sacks full of hair were stacked beside the door. Two sour-faced attendants were employed full-time shearing away at the ever-growing substance that was once her dead mother's pride and joy. The tight-lipped calmness of Rory Prince and his entourage reinforced her belief that she was quite mad. Sister Angela's warnings about the evils of money echoed in her head. Maybe she would smother herself quietly in her sleep. Edward the tea boy was becoming quite agile on the step ladder by this stage. He was even mildly friendly. From her perch Rapunzel could see down into the street below, people living normal everyday lives, unemployment queues, racing ambulances, and a lively demonstration in support of some political prisoner. She decided she would employ her time positively. Yes, that was it. She would systematically go through all her favourite composers ... Cole Porter, Irving Berlin, Peggy Seeger, Holly Near, that was it! At least she could annoy them with a few feminist songs.

Pauline's conversation with Rapunzel's neighbour scared her. Not a sign of her for five days. It was near finishing time when she reached Shineon Beauty Products Ltd. No, they had never heard of anyone by the name of Rapunzel Murphy. Perhaps if she came back tomorrow she could see the personnel manager. Pauline pushed her way through the tired workers as they emptied out of the lift. She swiftly worked her way through the maze of corridors. First floor, second floor. God, what an awful place to earn your living, she thought. On the seventh floor she narrowly avoided two security guards dressed in uniforms.

'Has Mr Snarl arrived yet?' one of them asked. 'Prince and Smarm and the other directors are waiting in the boardroom for an emergency sitting to assess the situation.'

Pauline slipped quickly into the fire stairs entrance. I must be near the top of the building, she thought. This is ridiculous. What am I doing here? I'll go to the police. I'll ring the Samaritans. I'll go to the Women's Centre! Oh it's so dry and hot. What the hell was that sound? *I'm a woman. W-O-M-A-N. Du be du du.'* Rapunzel! Two steps at a time is not fast enough, she thought, as she raced upstairs, through the next fire doors and into the plush, pink-coloured corridor lined with large refuse sacks. An over-powering smell of sweet synthetic soap met her. Rapunzel's voice was rising to a wild crescendo ... *'W-o-m-a-n and that's all. Du be du.'*

'She's drunk ... or drugged. She's gone over the top this time. Oh God! She was always so bloody artistic. This damned city!'

Kate White

Pauline tried the door. It was locked. 'Rapunzel,' she whispered. No answer came! 'Rapunzel!' she screamed. A door at the far end of the corridor opened and a thin, ashen-faced youth appeared with a tray. Pauline ducked around the corner and watched. The youth slowly opened the door as the first verse of *The Union Maid* started. While the door was closing behind him Pauline made a lurch at it, sending youth, cups, plates, hamburger and chips flying into the centre of the room.

'My God, Rapunzel, what have they done to you?' gasped Pauline, pushing her way through the mountains of hair. Shaking her head in disbelief, Pauline listened as Rapunzel revealed the horror of her ordeal over the last few days at the hands of Prince and his board of directors. Pauline's mind was working overtime: how to escape, how to expose the company for what they were ... She looked at the snivelling Edward, who was pathetically fiddling with the hair surrounding him, and suddenly she knew what to do.

'How long do these board meetings last?' she asked Edward, as she helped him up off the floor.

'Er ... um ... two or three hours at least,' he said.

'Good,' said Pauline. 'That gives us some time. Now, Rapunzel, you did an advanced weaving course last year. Do you think we could weave a web out of all this hair?'

'Well, I suppose I could, but I don't see ...'

'Never mind, just get cracking. Edward, can you help?'

'Yeah, sure, whatever you say,' said Edward, dusting himself off.

'Right, then, I'm going to find a phone and ring all the newspapers and the television as well and tell them to be here at eight o'clock for an urgent press conference. You stay here, Edward, and do what Rapunzel tells you. She'll teach you how to weave and you can help us to get out of here.'

'But what about my hair?' cried Rapunzel. 'They've tried everything to stop it and it's growing faster every day.'

'You leave that to me,' said Pauline, tapping the pocket of her jeans. 'I haven't spent the last two years working with herbs for nothing. Once we have the media here, I'll cut your hair and we'll apply some of my oil of herbina, which is so pure and uncontaminated it will counteract the effect of all those chemicals.'

Pauline dashed off to contact the press. Rapunzel began to teach Edward and, despite his clumsy fingers, they soon had a large and growing web flowing from their hands. Pauline returned, her face flushed with excitement. 'They're on their way,' she assured Rapunzel, 'and the television cameras will be here as well.'

'Great,' said Rapunzel, tying off the last of the knots in the web. Folding it carefully, she gave one end of it to Pauline and the other to Edward. They set off for the board-room, Rapunzel managing as best she could with five feet of hair trailing behind her. Quickly and quietly they ran down the fire stairs until they got to the seventh floor.

'Right, Edward, slip out there and check that the coast is clear,' instructed Pauline. 'Sure you're all right, Rapunzel?'

'Yes,' puffed Rapunzel, slightly out of breath. 'I'm glad I took up weightlifting this year. This hair weighs a ton.'

'It won't be long now,' smiled Pauline. 'You'll soon

have your revenge.'

'All clear,' whispered Edward. 'They're too busy arguing in there to hear a thing out here.'

'Just as well,' said Rapunzel as the lift doors opened. 'Here comes the press.'

As they crept nearer the boardroom they could hear the directors' voices.

'If this gets out, we could be ruined!' said one voice, 'I don't see that we have any other option.'

'I agree,' said another voice. 'We'll just have to get rid of her. It shouldn't be any problem. Don't forget, we picked a guinea pig without any nosy relatives.'

'I presume,' said another voice, 'that this will be one of our usual "accidents"?'

'Good God, no!' said a harsh voice. 'We can't even risk that. She will simply have to ... er ... disappear.'

Suddenly all was confusion. Rapunzel, Pauline and Edward burst into the room with the press hot on their heels. Before the startled board members could move, Rapunzel and Pauline flung the golden web over their astonished heads. With a flourish the two women turned to the assembled journalists.

'Here you have them, trapped in a web of their own making. This is the scoop of a lifetime. It's up to you to make sure they don't squirm out of this one.'

With that, Pauline turned to her friend and said, 'What about that trip to Donegal? I think we deserve it after all this.'

*Anne Claffey, Róisín Conroy,*
*Linda Kavanagh, Mary Paul Keane,*
*Catherine MacConville, Sue Russell.*

# Goldilocks Finds a Home

ONCE UPON A time in happy-ever-after land, deep in the Concrete Jungle, lived three bears. It was a typical nuclear family, Papa Bear, Mama Bear and the obligatory Baby Bear. With Papa Bear an upwardly mobile young executive type, they lacked none of the material comforts of a middle-class bear life. Their architect-designed, solar-powered house nestled amongst the trees, while their smaller, more compact town house was located in an up-market corner of Disenchantment Wood. Papa's pride and joy, the latest top-of-the-range Toyota model, nestled in the double garage beside Mama Bear's utilitarian but immaculate Mini. The kitchen, with all the latest appliances, was updated annually. Baby Bear's room was decorated as current trends dictated plenty of high-tech, educational, non-sexist toys.

However, amid all this comfort and convenience the Bears were careful not to neglect their social responsibilities. Papa Bear was a prominent member of his local Clean Street Campaign and consistently maintained his annual subscription to *Save the World Monthly Magazine*; Mama Bear dedicated two nights a week to various left-of-centre but socially acceptable groups. The Land Rights for Gay Whales and Vegies For All movements were typical examples, and Mama Bear could organise a sit-in, a phone-in or a fast-in at the drop of a hat.

It must be said at this point that Mama Bear was very careful not to neglect her family amidst all this activity. To Baby Bear she devoted one hour each day of intensive one-to-one interaction (whether Baby Bear felt like it or not). This, she thought, was what every bear needs, just as important as a healthy diet and stimulating lifestyle.

Every morning the three Bears, Papa Bear, Mama Bear and barely-conscious Baby Bear left the house for their two-kilometre jog through the forest. Before leaving the house, Mama Bear would prepare her special recipe apple juice, made from her own organically-grown apples, and lay a delicious bowl of sugar-free muesli ready for their return.

And so it happened that one fine June morning while they were out for their usual morning run, the lives of the three Bears were to be dramatically changed by circumstances beyond their control.

In another part of the Concrete Jungle someone else was out walking, but for a very different reason. Goldilocks (so called, since a freak accident with a bottle of peroxide) McCarthy was out for a walk to try to clear her head. Life in the last few months had been a nightmare for Goldilocks. Home had become a prison with her father the jailer. His had been a prison of the mind; he was too clever to use force. Bruises on the outside were easily seen, but mental scars were harder to see and harder to heal. She and her mother had thought it just a sign of the times at first, a tightening of the belt, watching the pennies to mind the pounds. But soon it was not just money that had to be accounted for, but time as well. It had been horrible to watch him tightening his grip, taking complete control of everything and everyone around him, their time, their money, their lives.

It had taken all her mother's resources to pack her bags, take the children and go. Go where? That was the question. Where does a married woman with three children and no money go? Staying with Aunt Liz was fine for now, but they were living on top of each other and sooner or later he would find them out.

Goldilocks trudged on deeper into the Concrete Jungle, tired, hungry and worn out from worry. Walking along with her head down she was nearly run over by a family of enthusiastic joggers. That's funny, she thought, I didn't know that there were bears living this far out. But she dismissed them from her mind and walked on. Try as she could, Goldilocks could not see a solution to her problem and was just about to turn back, when suddenly in a clearing just ahead she caught a glimpse of a magnificent house.

The first thing Goldilocks noticed about it was the garden. It was a children's wonderland. It had every conceivable kind of toy, swings, roundabouts, climbing frames, slides, the lot. Enough to keep twenty children occupied. But where were the children? There wasn't sign or light of anyone around the place and everything looked brand new. Goldilocks couldn't resist a quick go on the swings. She felt happy again as she swung higher and higher. It had been a long time since she had let go like this. Better be careful, she thought, this swing won't take my weight for much longer, and indeed as she jumped off she saw that the seat was slightly bent. Oh well, she said to herself, at least it's been used.

Still puzzled by the lack of signs of life, Goldilocks drew nearer to the house. She had never been so close to such a large house before. The garage alone was probably as big as the house where she and her family were living at present. Looking around rapidly, she decided to risk a quick peek through one of the windows. She could not believe her eyes. In the middle of the most perfect kitchen, with gleaming equipment and space enough to feed an army, was a table laid for breakfast, and only three places set! With hunger rumbling in her stomach she could almost taste the food and smell the coffee which was bubbling away on the hob. Before she could make a move, however, she heard footsteps approaching through the forest. Quickly she jumped down and took cover behind the sandpit, determined to see who lived there.

It was Baby Bear who noticed something amiss as he returned from his run.

'Someone's been swinging on my swing,' he said, 'and it's all bent. Look!'

'Don't be silly,' said Mama Bear. `There's no one around here for miles. Now come inside and eat your breakfast, there's a good boy.'

Being a well-brought-up little bear, he did as he was told.

As she made her way back home, Goldilocks pondered life's injustices. To think of her mother, herself and two other children all crowded into Aunt Liz's tiny house, while those three bears were rattling around in that huge house. More than ever she determined to do something to change the situation.

First, she sought help from the local Concrete Jungle Housing Bureau. The waiting list for houses was endless. The bear in charge was totally unsympathetic and suggested to Goldilocks that she and her mother go back home like good little girls and not cause

trouble. Looking around the office, it seemed to Goldilocks that this was the general advice given to women in that situation. Most of the women looked tired and weary and ready to give up. A roof over their heads, a bite to eat and somewhere for the children to play; it's little enough to ask, thought Goldilocks ... Somewhere for the children to play ... Suddenly it hit her ... I know where there's a place for our family and a few more besides. Now if only ...

Goldilocks drew up a plan of action. She watched the three Bears' house every morning for a week and saw that they never changed their routine. Once or twice she even went inside and tasted the food and checked out the number of bedrooms. Baby Bear seemed to be the only one who noticed. Mama and Papa Bear were oblivious and paid no attention to Baby Bear's remarks about missing bowls of muesli. Maybe they just don't know what's going on out here in the Jungle, thought Goldilocks. They mustn't realise how different things are for the rest of us.

She contacted her local Housing Action Group, as well as her women's group, and talked to them about her plan. It was quite straightforward as far as she could see. The three Bears had two houses, both of which were far too big for their own needs; she and the others had no house at all. So?

The plan was simple. Goldilocks, her mother and sisters and two other homeless single mothers would install themselves in the house while the three Bears were out running through the forest. They would offer the Bears a choice: they could either move in to their town house in Disenchantment Wood or they could all live together as a community. Goldilocks' mother expressed doubts about living with the Bears. She hadn't got out of the frying pan only to leap into the fire. But Goldilocks assured her that the Bears were quite harmless really, and would possibly be taken with the idea of a commune.

And so it happened. The plan worked like a dream. On the appointed day the three Bears went jogging as usual, quite oblivious of what was in store for them. In went Goldilocks and friends. They prepared to blockade the doors in case the Bears got nasty and called in the Grizzlies. But they need not have worried. Although slightly taken aback at having their home taken over, Mama Bear and Papa Bear took it pretty well. When Papa Bear expressed a little dismay at having to move the Toyota to make room in the garage for extra storage space, Mama was quick to remind him of the article in last month's *Planet Savers Today* about communes. It would be quite an experience to actually live in a real commune instead of just reading about it. And anyway, she whispered, we can always go to the town house if things get a bit much here.

Baby Bear remained the only fly in the ointment. He was absolutely horrified at the idea of having to share his toys and space. He threw a huge tantrum, until Mama Bear, totally perplexed at his behaviour, actually shouted at him to calm down. Baby Bear got such a shock that he stopped in his tracks, speechless. He too began to see that things would never be the same again in the woods.

*Sue Russell*

# Some Day My Prince Will Come

Some day my prince will come
And carry me away
But my social life's so hectic
I just hope I'm in that day.

*Róisín Sheerin*

Paula Nolan

# The Princesses' Forum

ONCE UPON A time, all the princesses and heroines of fairy tales got together at Snow White's cottage to discuss the shortage of intelligent princes.

'I've decided that there's no point in hanging around my place, waiting for some idiot to force his way through the thicket,' said Sleeping Beauty (who was really quite wide awake).

'And *I'm* sick of that lunatic with the foot fetish,' said Cinderella. 'Imagine selecting your life partner on the basis of her shoe size? How could any self-respecting woman cope with a man like that?'

'After keeping house for seven dwarfs,' said Snow White, 'I never want to see another man again. Not one of them ever put the cap back on the toothpaste or washed their smelly socks.'

'I know exactly what you mean,' said Rapunzel. 'The one who came courting me wasn't very bright. Can you imagine it? Being trapped at the top of a tower, unable to escape. I was delighted when this fellow climbed up. I was sure my days as a prisoner were over. But the fool climbed down again! Each time he came back, he promised to bring a ladder with him the next time. But he kept on forgetting.'

'Forgetting, my foot!' said Cinderella (who had feet on the brain). 'I just hope for your sake you're not in any trouble.'

'In trouble?' said Rapunzel, looking surprised. 'How could I be in trouble? Since the day you all rescued me,

I've been in great form. I'm eating like a horse and I've put on half a stone in weight ... '

'What ?' shrieked all the princesses and heroines in unison. 'Did you say "half a stone in weight"?'

'Yes,' said Rapunzel in happy innocence. 'But there's just one teeny weeny problem which one of you might be able to advise me about. Lately, I always seem to feel queasy in the mornings ...'

She looked askance as the others fell about the place in consternation.

'To think that we got together to discuss the shortage of princes ...' groaned Snow White.

' ... and already, there's been one prince too many,' finished Sleeping Beauty crossly.

'Well, there's only one thing to do,' said Cinderella, 'and that is to take her to Red Riding Hood's grandmother in the forest. She's an expert in dealing with this kind of situation. I'll take her there immediately after this meeting.'

Rapunzel sat silently, bewildered at the response that had been generated by her comments. She made a mental note to keep quiet in future.

'Right,' said Snow White, bringing the meeting back to order. 'We were discussing the princes. Since the only ones available are an unimpressive lot, what are we going to do?'

'It's all very well for *you*,' said Goldilocks. 'I've *never* had a prince of my own. Being chased by three bears is no fun, you know. I'd prefer a boor to a bear any day.'

'I agree,' said Rapunzel, breaking her self-imposed rule of silence. 'I think ...'

'If I were you,' said Cinderella, looking directly at her, 'I'd keep my big mouth shut.'

'Order, order,' called Snow White. 'I repeat, what are

we going to do?'

'I think we're all victims of stereotyping,' said Red Riding Hood. 'Everyone assumes that in order to live happily ever after, we must each have a prince in tow. Give me a fine specimen of wolfhound any day. Or a woodcutter,' she added, lowering her eyes and blushing happily at the recent memory.

'I don't see why we need to have princes at all,' said Sleeping Beauty. 'I'm not particularly keen to have some idiot come along and try to annexe my territory to his, under the guise of having fallen madly in love with me.'

'But princesses *have* to marry, and it *has* to be a prince,' said Goldilocks. 'Otherwise, there'll be no heirs to the kingdom, and ...'

'*King*dom,' repeated Cinderella. 'Now, *there's* a word I object to. Why shouldn't it be Queendom?'

'I suppose it's like the word "man",' said Red Riding Hood. 'It's meant to cover both men and women.'

'Well, I for one, object to being called a man,' said the Sleeping Beauty. 'I don't even look like one, do I?'

'I'm tired of having to behave like a princess,' said Snow White. 'I'm not delicate, I'm not silly and I'm certainly not weak. Anyone who could keep house for seven little chauvinists,  and not lose their sanity, has to be a very strong person.'

'Have you noticed,' said Sleeping Beauty suddenly, 'that in many of our stories, our enemies are other women?'

'That's because men wrote the stories,' said Cinderella. 'It makes them feel good to have women fighting among themselves for male attention.'

'Well then,' said the Sleeping Beauty, 'we'll just have to re-write the stories ourselves. I'd just love to rescue some good-looking fellow who's been imprisoned in a castle or tower by a wicked uncle or stepfather.'

'That's a ridiculous plot,' said Goldilocks contemptuously.

'I know,' said Sleeping Beauty, 'but it's actually the plot of *our* stories in reverse.'

'I hope we're not just going to reverse the situation,' said Cinderella. 'In that event, we'd only be reversing the role of oppressor and oppressed. I don't want to oppress anyone.'

All the women nodded agreement.

'The first change I want to make,' said Snow White, 'is to get my stepmother the Queen on our side. Once we're not in competition for men's approval, it won't matter which of us is better-looking. Then she'll have no reason to be jealous of me any more. Besides, she's a very brilliant woman, with her laboratories downstairs in the castle dungeon. I'm sure I could convince her to develop the science of pharmacology for good rather than evil.'

'When you think of it,' said Cinderella, 'there will be no need for other women to be our enemies if we're not fighting over who gets those macho idiots. What fun we could all have together instead!'

At that precise moment (as always conveniently happens in fairytales) three princes arrived at the door. They had been on an ego trip through the forest, looking for dragons to fight or helpless princesses to rescue.

Seeing Cinderella peering out at them from one of the cottage windows, their eyes lit up with delight. The first one gave an exaggerated bow and nearly fell off his horse. 'Hi there, gorgeous!' shouted the second one. 'Do you need to be rescued?' shouted the third one.

Cinderella's reply was certainly not the type of language normally attributed to demure princesses.

'Invite them in,' said Snow White, nudging her in the ribs. 'I think we should let them know we're writing them out of the scripts.'

The princes looked bewildered as they were ushered into the room full of princesses and heroines. They were used to ogling females one at a time, but a whole room full of them was just too daunting a prospect.

Quickly, Cinderella explained the discussions that had taken place and the conclusions the women had reached. 'So you see,' she finished, 'we're not very impressed with all that macho stuff.'

The three princes looked from one to the other in astonishment. 'Do you mean that we don't need to be big, strong and fearless any more?' asked the first one.

'Do you mean that princesses are *not* all frail and helpless?' asked the second one.

'Yes to both questions,' said Snow White. 'We're tired of behaving the way stereotyped princesses are supposed to. We're going to behave as *we* want from now on.'

Once again, the princes looked from one to the other, mopping their brows in unison. 'Phew,' said the first one.

'What a relief!' said the second one.

'That's the best news I've heard,' said the third prince. 'I'm tired of always feeling under pressure to be brave and fearless. I get awfully scared sometimes, but I've never been able to tell anyone else. I thought I was the only man who ever felt that way.'

PRINCESSES' FORUM

Siobhán Condon

The second prince said, 'It's such a relief to be able to act naturally. I was terrified at the thought of having to battle my way through those enormous briars around Sleeping Beauty's castle. Do you really mean that I don't have to do that any more?'

'Definitely not,' said Sleeping Beauty. 'You can call to the door like any normal civilised visitor, as soon as I get all those briars cleared away and the palace cleaned up.'

'Let's all come round to your place next week,' said Goldilocks. 'Together, we could have the job done in an afternoon.'

Everyone nodded in agreement, including the three princes.

Meanwhile, Cinderella had managed to sit down beside the second prince. 'I think you're cute!' she whispered, 'I wouldn't mind writing *you* into my new script.'

The prince turned scarlet but looked very pleased nevertheless. 'I wouldn't mind either,' he said timidly.

Just then, there was a loud hammering on the cottage door, and another prince, carrying a ladder, was ushered into the room. His initial bewilderment gave way to delight when he saw Rapunzel. 'Darling!' he cried.

'Precious!' she answered, and they rushed into each other's arms.

'I was really worried ...' murmured the prince '... when you weren't in the tower. I'd planned *such* a romantic escape.'

'Well,' said Snow White, 'at least he's had the decency to turn up.'

'Do you realise,' said Cinderella, tapping him on the shoulder, 'that you've got this poor creature pregnant?'

Rapunzel and her prince both looked astonished.

'But I thought ...' began the prince.

'What on earth do you mean?' asked Rapunzel angrily. 'I think you've got a nerve.'

'Well,' said Snow White, 'you said yourself you've put on half a stone in weight.'

'That's because I've been taking the pill,' said Rapunzel crossly. 'You don't think we'd start a deep, meaningful relationship without being responsible about it?'

The gathering of princesses and heroines gave an audible sigh of relief.

Just then the door creaked open, and a snout with large gleaming fangs appeared. Cinderella pulled open the door, and a huge hairy wolf fell into their midst.

'What on earth are you doing here?' said Red Riding Hood crossly.

'Sorry,' said the wolf, rising to his feet. 'I was just looking for someone to eat. It's way past dinner time, and I'm absolutely starving.'

'Look here,' said Cinderella, 'this kind of carry-on just isn't acceptable any more. We've decided to re-write all the fairy tales, and if you're not going to behave civilly, we'll write you out of the Red Riding Hood story altogether.'

'Oh, please don't do that,' said the wolf miserably. 'I only eat people because I can't afford to buy food. Wealthy people like yourselves never give a thought to the plight of the poor.'

The group was silent for a moment, then Cinderella spoke. 'Perhaps we could remedy the situation by having some kind of regular payment for those who don't earn enough money to live on,' she said, turning to the wolf. 'Will you promise to give up eating people, if this can be arranged?'

'Wolf's honour,' said the wolf, holding up his right forepaw. 'Quite honestly, I prefer the tinned or frozen stuff. People tend to give me indigestion anyway ...'

The group rose to its feet, and everyone began to prepare for their departure from the cottage.

'I'm going home to have a serious talk with my stepsisters,' said Cinderella to Goldilocks, as she put on her cloak. 'I did an assertiveness training course recently, and I learned how to stand up for myself in the face of those two bullies. *My* days of being tied to the kitchen sink are definitely over.'

'Good for you,' said Goldilocks approvingly, 'and please tell us where you did the course. I think *I* need something like that to deal with those three aggressive bears.'

Outside the castle, Sleeping Beauty was sitting astride her horse. 'Are you fellows okay?' she asked looking down at the three rather forlorn-looking princes, who were standing, typically, apart from the women.

'Of course,' replied the first prince, puffing out his chest. Then he remembered what had transpired at the meeting. 'Well ... er ... no, actually,' he confessed. 'To be perfectly honest, now that we're all going to be honest with each other, that is, I'm really quite frightened at the thought of going home alone through the dark forest.' The other two princes nodded in assent.

'Don't worry,' said Sleeping Beauty. 'I'm passing your place on my way home. You'll be quite safe with me.'

'Besides,' added Snow White from the cottage doorway, 'there'll be nothing to be afraid of any more, if the wolf, the witches and the dragons are all our friends.'

Cinderella approached the second prince. 'If you're worried going home alone, ' she whispered, 'I'll go with you and hold your hand.'

The second prince and Cinderella disappeared into the woods together.

'Goodbye, everyone,' called Goldilocks and Red Riding Hood, as they headed off together down the woodland path.

'Don't forget,' Sleeping Beauty called after them, 'my place next week! When the briars are cleared away, we'll have a sing-song and a few bottles of wine. Is everyone agreed?'

'Sounds great,' said the first prince.

'Have you any whisky?' asked the third prince hopefully.

The wolf was too busy feasting at Snow White's table to reply. But he did manage to grunt in agreement.

Rapunzel and her prince smiled dreamily in assent, hardly able to think of anything but each other.

When they had all gone home, Snow White closed the cottage door, and headed off to talk to her stepmother about this recent upturn in events. Perhaps, she thought, they *would* all live happily ever after.

*Linda Kavanagh*

# Hi Ho, It's Off To Strike We Go!

THERE WAS once a young woman who was clever and kind, serious and witty. On top of all that, her family was wildly wealthy. Her name was Margaret, which is a perfectly useful name to have. But, of course, it is the way of families to give their members nicknames. Since she was born on the night of a dreadful blizzard, somebody or other decided to call her 'Snow White', and one way or another the name stuck, although for most of the time the family just used 'Snow', as in 'Snow, your tea is ready!'

Apart from this bit of foolishness, there was little in the world to trouble our Snow during the years of her childhood, which she spent playing and romping, reading and thinking and turning over new ideas, just like most clever, kind, serious and witty young women. All would have gone blissfully forever, if it hadn't been for her mother.

'I'm fed up looking at you playing and romping and reading and thinking and turning over new ideas,' Snow's mother said to her one day. 'Why don't you get a job?'

'Oh, mother, you are wicked,' Snow sighed. 'Anyway, there are no jobs. There's a recession, as you know very well.'

'Just the same, it's time you did something. If you go on hanging around here, what's to become of you?

44

First thing you know, the hall will be cluttered with handsome suitors looking for your hand in marriage, and the next thing you'll pick out one of them to fall in love with, and within a year and a day, you'll be well on the way to ending up like myself. Look how your father made his money. Manufacturing Magic Mirrors. Do you know what the secret of Magic Mirrors' success is? Behind every mirror is a sheet of rosy pink, and every woman who looks into one thinks she's the fairest of them all. Small good it does any of us, I can tell you. Looking at yourself in a rose-tinted mirror is worse than looking at the world through glasses of the same hue, my girl, and I want you to make something of yourself.'

'Hmm,' said Snow. 'But if you're restless, mother, why not take a re-training course for yourself? I'm sure there's something you could learn to do.'

After that, her mother sent her packing for cheek, and so it was that Snow White went off in search of her fortune, or at least, a job. But there was a recession, of course, and truth to tell, she couldn't find anything that suited her, which is why she finally ended up answering an ad for a housekeeper in a tiny mining village.

She was interviewed by seven short, gnarled men who had a long and tedious list of chores she was meant to do each day: washing, cooking, sweeping, making beds, and so on. It sounded dreadful and the wages were pretty poor. But Snow White took the job, all the time privately wondering why seven men couldn't share out the housework among themselves.

By the time she had finished her first week's work, Snow White had her answer. The seven miners worked sixteen hours a day in the Prince Precious Jewel Mining

Company, and were so exhausted at night they could barely scoff down the lovely porridge she had cooked for them.

'For pity's sake,' Snow White asked them when she had her wages on Friday night, 'haven't you ever heard of the trade union movement?'

'No,' said the little miner named Dopey. 'Tell us the story, Snow White.'

So Snow White told them all about capital and exploitation and unity being strength and free collective bargaining, and on Monday morning the seven miners marched into Mr Prince and demanded shorter working hours, meal breaks, a rise in wages and a pension plan. When they had made all their demands, Mr Prince and the Prince Precious Jewel Mining Company told them they could take a running jump with themselves, so they trooped back to Snow White.

'What will we do now?' asked the miner named Sleepy, stifling a yawn,

'We will go on strike,' said Snow White. 'That ought to wake things up around here.'

So Snow White organised the seven little miners into picketing shifts and got everyone into painting slogans on posters such as 'Precious little from Precious Jewel' and 'Prince pays poorly.' For three days and three nights the seven miners took it in turn to picket the mines, and Snow White took the fellows who were off picket duty and gave them a crash course in washing, cooking, sweeping and so on. She had some plans of her own at this point, you see.

On the third night, Mr Prince met the seven little miners and said 'All right, all right, I'll discuss your demands. This strike is costing me a dragon's ransom

Siobhán Condon

in unmined rubies and emeralds and diamonds.' So Snow White took the seven little miners aside and told them to put their demands all over again, but to add on that they wanted at least one more worker.

'In fact, better say two more workers,' she advised. 'And for that matter, name a higher wage increase than you will settle for, and a better pension plan than you are looking for, and ask for five meal breaks instead of three. Industrial relations are only human relations, and must be negotiated.'

Eventually, the miners and Mr Prince worked out a settlement, and not a minute too soon either, because the porridge pot was running dry. 'Great news,' Snow

47

White said briskly when the miners came back with the jubilant information that they had won. 'Now there'll be enough money again for porridge. One of you had better go out and buy some, because as of this minute, I am applying for a job as a miner.'

Off she went to Mr Prince's office. Now Mr Prince was a likeable enough fellow and was, for his own part, kind and serious, occasionally witty and bright enough, but weighed down with a lot of prejudices.

'Don't be absurd,' he told Snow White. 'This is no sort of work for a girl.'

'Why not?' asked Snow White. 'I'm not afraid of the dark and I have done my share of digging during the days when I was playing and romping and all that.'

'But you are beautiful,' Mr Prince said, 'and everyone knows that the right place for a beautiful girl is in the reception office, so how about a nice desk job, receiving visitors to the Prince Precious Jewel Company?'

'As for that, personal comments have no place in the workplace,' Snow White said. 'However, I'll consider the receptionist job provided, naturally, that the pay is the same as the male miners get.'

At that, Mr Prince knew he was defeated and meekly agreed to send Snow White down to the mines. After all, he could always find some other pretty little girl to take the job in the front office. 'Oh, and by the way,' Snow White said as she left the office, 'my union is keeping a sharp eye out for underpaid female labour. We wouldn't hesitate to strike again on behalf of someone you hire for the front office, if you don't pay properly.'

So it was that Snow White took up her shovel and pick and went down the mines. She also took care to see that the Precious Jewel Miners' Union promptly affiliated to all the other unions on the mountain, and succeeded in being elected chief shop steward at the first meeting of the Mountainside Miners' Associated Unions. She set about negotiating with the bosses, ogres and princes on a wide range of benefits. She won protective safety wear, paid holidays, a sick pay scheme, grievance and appointments procedures and a positive action programme for all females employed on the mountain. She saw to it that the different managements set up subsidised canteens so as to eliminate all that porridge stirring, and insisted on crêches as a matter of principle, though they were not yet required. 'They will be,' she assured Mr Prince and the other bosses firmly.

One night Mr Prince approached Snow White and asked if she was possibly free for dinner. 'I have a proposal I'd like to make to you,' he said shyly.

'I'll have to clear it with the union committee first,' Snow White answered, 'but I don't think they will object.'

Mr Prince took her to the nicest restaurant on the mountainside and asked what she'd like to eat. 'Anything but bloody porridge,' Snow White said, scanning the menu. 'Let's see, what about Terrine de Campagne, followed by Tournedos Medici and dessert?'

'Certainly,' said Mr Prince, 'with a nice bottle of champagne to follow.'

The meal went beautifully until the end, when Mr Prince decided to order just cheese and a bit of fruit for afters. Snow White, being a sensible woman, had apricot torte with almonds and was just tucking into it when Mr Prince bit into his apple, choked and fell into a swoon.

Well, this threw everyone into a nice tizzy, as you can imagine. 'A swoon, a swoon, and I can't remember the words of one decent spell,' the owner of the restaurant kept shouting. Other customers tried out spells they could recall, and one or two said a spell in jail is what fellows who drank too much deserved.

Snow White, however, considered the situation, and picked Mr Prince up by the heels, bending one arm expertly underneath his knees in a hold she had learned in karate class. She delivered one swift karate blow between his shoulder blades and, lo and behold, out came the bit of apple.

'There y'are now, not a bother on you,' Snow White said when Mr Prince opened his eyes. 'I think we'd better be getting home, though, just to be on the safe side. What was it you wanted to propose to me?'

Mr Prince gazed at her with admiration and respect. 'I wanted to propose that you become my partner,' he said softly.

Snow White dusted off his suit, put his plumed hat back on his head and signalled a passing white steed to carry them off into the night.

'Only on one condition,' she said.

'Anything,' Mr Prince replied, his voice trembling.

'It would have to be a workers' co-op, and the unions would have to support my membership on the board. I'm sure we could devise suitable structures. I'll have to take a look at the EC directives. It's certainly worth considering, and I am very interested in industrial democracy. It's about time we began taking over. Lovely meal, wasn't it? Apart, of course, from the apple.'

*Mary Maher*

# Jack's Mother and The Beanstalk

'AH WELL, you have to speculate to accumulate,' sighed Jack's mother when Jack came home with the bag of beans. 'That's the first rule in business.'

She wondered sometimes whether it was wise to try to teach Jack the rudiments of business administration. It seemed to confuse him and gave him headaches. More in hope than in anticipation she planted the beans outside their little cottage and went back to reading the *Financial Times*.

All night the beanstalk grew until in the morning it reached the sky.

'Keep my dinner warm in the oven, Jack,' Jack's mother said, putting on a pair of her dead husband's breeches before starting her climb up the beanstalk.

'MOTHER!' screeched Jack when he saw her. 'You can't go out dressed like that. What'll the neighbours think?'

'We don't have any neighbours,' Jack's mother said and continued to climb.

When she reached the top of the beanstalk she found herself on a path that led eventually to a tall castle. Tired and hungry she let herself in and helped herself to some soup that was bubbling on the stove. Afterwards she fell asleep in a cupboard.

When she awoke it was dark. She peeped out through a crack in the door. At the table sat an enormous giant who was shovelling food into his mouth. He looked vaguely familiar but she could not think why. Suddenly he stopped eating and sniffed loudly. In a voice that made the castle shake he roared:

*Fee fi fo fum*
*I smell the blood of an Englishman*
*Be he alive or be he dead*
*I'll grind his bones to make my bread.*

'Well, that's the limit!' thought Jack's mother and leapt out of her hiding place. 'It's one thing calling me English. I could forgive that,' she shouted, boxing the giant hard on the ears. 'But it's another thing to say that I smell like a man, you male chauvinist giant.' She gave him an almighty punch on the nose.

'That's not fair,' he shouted back.

'Yes it is, ' she snarled.

'No it isn't. I've never discriminated,' the giant said in an injured tone. 'Man or woman, I'll eat either.'

The giant and Jack's mother glared at each other and then the giant began to chase her around the castle, up and down stairs, in and out of rooms until the giant collapsed into a chair clutching his chest. (He had a weak heart - the result of too much protein in his diet. Eating people isn't just wrong, dear reader, it's also bad for your health.) She climbed on to a window ledge and looked at him closely.

Finally she spoke: 'I know you. You came into my office when I worked as an investment consultant before I married that good-for-nothing farmer. You ran a business - Giant Inc. I even invested in it myself. Two grand I put in and then you did a bunk. You low-down, lily-livered rat!' She looked around the room. 'You did all right for yourself though, I'll say that for you. Lovely pad you've got. A quick inventory and I'll tell you how much you're worth.'

Jack's mother took out a notebook and began to write. 'Nice work, giant,' she complimented him when she had totted up the figures. 'You've got some good antiques. Great pictures too. Originals. I like them. Now I'll work out my percentage and take my cut.'

'But I'm a *giant*,' wailed the giant. 'From me you're supposed to flee in fear.'

'From me a flea in your ear,' Jack's mother snapped back. 'Keep quiet. I'm calculating.' To show she meant business she dug her biro between his ribs. The giant groaned and covered his eyes.

'Taking interest into account,' Jack's mother continued, 'plus accumulated profit I reckon you owe me nine million, fourteen thousand, three hundred and twenty-five pounds. Seeing as you're an old friend, I'll leave off the twenty- five pounds.'

The giant breathed heavily. He seemed to be recovering his strength. Quickly Jack's mother surveyed the room. Her attention was caught by the sight of a hen that was sitting on a clutch of golden eggs. 'Now there's a good investment,' she said admiringly as she scooped the hen into her arms. 'I'll take her as part payment.'

In the corner a magical harp was playing mournfully to itself.

'I adore music,' said Jack's mother. 'I'll take the harp as the rest of the payment.'

'Oh heaven,' twanged the harp gratefully as Jack's mother escaped out of the door, the harp in one hand, the hen in the other. 'At last, I've someone who appreciates me. You can't imagine what hell it's been living with that giant. All he ever listens to is James Last and Barry Manilow.'

*Siobhán Condon*

Jack's mother was too busy running down the path to reply. With the giant in hot pursuit she began to climb down the beanstalk. 'Get the axe!' she hollered to Jack. 'This is an example of asset-stripping,' she informed him as, womanfully, she swung the axe at the beanstalk. Within seconds the beanstalk came crashing down around them. 'Chop it up,' she instructed Jack, handing him the axe. 'We'll sell the pieces for firewood. We won't make much on it but no venture is too small - that's the second rule of business, Jack.'

Thanks to the hen that laid the golden eggs, the magical harp and Jack's mother's business acumen, Jack and his mother lived happily and prosperously ever after.

Jack never got the hang of business administration but then, he didn't need to !

*Elizabeth O'Driscoll*

# The Fate of Aoife and the Children of Aobh

THIS IS THE story of two sisters, their children and the fate brought upon them by the jealousy and dominance of warring men and how one sister, Aoife, transformed that fate.

It is a story that has been told many times but the full truth has not yet been set down.

In the age of the Tuatha De Danaan, after the battle of Tailltin, there was a rivalry between two Kings; Bodb Dearg and Lir of the Hill of the White Fields whom he defeated for the Lordship.

Now it happened that Lir's wife died after an illness and Bodb Dearg, wanting to placate Lir and win his fealty, offered him as a bride Aobh, the eldest of his three foster daughters. And Lir accepted and married her, pleased not only by Aobh's beauty and high birth but also by the influence the marriage brought him.

In the course of time a daughter, Fionnuala, was born to Aobh and later a son. It was not until many years later, however, when these children were well grown that she conceived again, this time giving birth to twin boys; Fiachra and Conn. But in giving them life she forfeited her own.

All the people of the land keened Aobh. And when Bodb Dearg learnt of it he too mourned her. For he had been proud of Aobh and well satisfied with the loyalty she had won from his son-in-law. So when in due time he was told that Lir was once more looking for a wife, in order to maintain that friendship, he announced that he would make him a gift of another woman: Aobh's younger sister Aoife.

Lir was flattered and more than pleased to find a wife so quickly with so little trouble to himself. He had felt the loss of Aobh and needed a mother for his four children.

But there was no joy in Aoife's heart when she discovered what was being planned for her: that she was to marry this ageing man who had buried two wives already, the second her own sister. She knew little of him that could not be said of her father and brothers, and for all she knew, of most men; that he was courageous in battle, shrewd in the conduct of his affairs, a proud, possessive man who loved wine and horses above all else. One consideration however, outweighed the rest, one he and her father knew nothing of. When Aobh was dying she had sent for Aoife, the sister with whom she had from the first days of their fosterage a special bond and, taking her hand, had asked her to promise that should she die, Aoife would love and protect her four children as if they were her own. And Aoife, weeping, had given her promise.

So when Lir came to her father's court with his chariots and retinue she married him and returned to his household.

And it was a strange thing for the young Aoife to live in the house she had known as her sister's guest, to find herself mistress of that household. It was strange and painful to walk in the gardens, eat at the table, sleep in the bed that had been her sister's. Everything she did reminded her of Aobh and increased her sense of loss. But one consolation she had, and it was an abundant one: the company of the children, Fionnuala, Aodh, Fiachra and Conn. These four were said to be the most beautiful in Ireland. No one seeing them could resist enchantment. And it was not only beauty they possessed but grace, intelligence and a rare sweetness of nature.

Every hour of the day they played together, the four children and their step-mother, and in their lightness of heart and gaiety they were more like five children than four. In the woods and rivers of the White Fields they ran like fawns or wild young horses; in the evening they gathered by the fires of the great hall to tell stories and listen to the music of Aoife's harp.

Lir saw little of them. A lord and warrior, his affairs required much journeying; administering his lands, dealing with his subjects, playing chess with rival chieftains, hunting deer and fishing salmon. But when he was at home he felt the new mood of festivity in the house. And seeing the delight his wife and young children had in each other's company, he was torn between excitement and jealousy. Proud beyond sense of their beauty, he would snatch up his small sons, one in each fist, and wave them high in the air, and Fionnuala he would take galloping on horseback, holding her before him, her red-gold hair blowing about her to exhibit to all who passed.

One day, saying that with all his travel he was too much deprived of his children, he ordered the servants to make their beds in the room next to his. From then on every night before sleeping he would steal in to gaze upon them and in the morning so exuberant and possessive was his affection that immediately upon waking he would go in to their room and lie down

57

with them.

In the spring of that year Aoife found she was with child. As her time drew near she was frightened, being so young and remembering the pain it had cost her sister. Lir, however, was overjoyed for it was the one thing left for him to want; a child of their new union to show that he was not yet an old man. But though the birth did not cost Aoife what it had cost Aobh, the infant was born early and born dead. It was mourned and buried while Lir was away in another kingdom. When he returned and learnt what had happened he was taken by a fit of rage that put fear in all who saw it. He went straight to Aoife and finding her lying white-faced and exhausted, it was not pity or tenderness he felt but an increase of anger. He berated her with a ferocity she had not known before. He accused her of carelessness. If she had not insisted on sporting and playing with his children as if she was a child herself, he said, instead of a mother, this blight would not have come upon them. And he went from the room cursing her.

It was bitter beyond knowing for Aoife to be blamed for the death that was her greatest sorrow.

A coldness came between them from that day forward. Lir's journeys became more frequent and prolonged. When he was at home he avoided Aoife and spoke little to her. But though he shunned his wife he was more than ever possessive of his sons and daughter. He would sit late into the night feasting and drinking with his warriors and when at last he rose for sleep it was not to Aoife's room he went but to the children's. He boasted of them hourly and demanded their company at every moment, but a harshness and

Paula Nolan

discontent entered his affection so that no matter how they studied to please him he was never satisfied.

Aoife saw this and was frightened. She thought it was his anger with her that corrupted his feeling. She saw how he petted and made much of Fionnuala, wooing her praise as if only it could restore his self-esteem. But she believed she had no power to influence him, hostile and resentful as he had become to her.

The time arrived when she must make a visit to her foster parents. Not wanting to leave, weary still from the death of the child, she nonetheless made her preparations. Fionnuala came to her, who nearest in age was closest to her heart. She asked Aoife not to leave her alone with Lir, who was so demanding of her. Aoife soothed her and promised a swift return. And setting out she left the children in their father's care.

She was absent from them seven weeks and in that time there was not an hour that she did not think of them. At last, her strength renewed, she departed from Bodb Dearg's kingdom and began her journey to the White Fields. As she drove past Loch Dairbhreach she felt a sudden apprehension and she could not persuade the horses to go quickly enough. When she approached the palace there was a strange quiet to it. Lir was away from home, his dogs and horses and servants gone with him. She stood in the courtyard and called for Fionnuala and Aodh but they did not answer. She called the names of Fiachra and Conn and silence remained. She searched the house for them and at length found them quiet together in the furthest room of the house. When she saw the fear in their eyes she was afraid to question them. She stood hesitant on the threshold and they ran to her and threw themselves into her arms, weeping. That evening she talked alone to Fionnuala and discovered what she already feared and what Fionnuala scarcely had words to tell her. Their father had come late from the table every night after heavy drinking, laughing and crying at once, lamenting his dead wife and child, had come to her room and slept in her bed. And Fionnuala, though hardly more than a child herself, was with child and its father was her own father, Lir of the Hill of the White Fields.

Hearing this, pain went through Aoife's breast like a sword. The children she loved above life, whose protection she had been charged with, she had left uncared for, unguarded. And was it not her fault if this great harm had come to them?

But what was she to do? Could she pit herself against Lir?

Lir who had a man's power and a king's power and a husband's power. What had she to set against these?

She bade the children to dress and prepare for a journey. She knew if it was to be done she must leave at once before any soul guessed her thought, before she lost her courage and resolution for it. Putting a dagger to the left of her cloak and a druid wand to the right of it and taking food enough for three days, they set out in one chariot.

They travelled without rest until nightfall. They slept in the forest and woke at first light. At first Aoife had thought of seeking refuge in her father's kingdom, but as they drew near his land she knew it held no sanctuary for her. It was to Lir his loyalty was pledged. He would not believe her story. They would call her an unnatural woman who stole her husband's children out of jealousy.

Later that day they stopped to eat by a river and learnt from some woodsmen that Lir of the White Fields was pursuing, with a great troop of horses, the wife who had carried off his children. And Lir's heart, they said, 'was a core of hatred for her and when he found this woman no punishment would be fit for her'.

Terror gripped Aoife and despair at her helplessness. She called the children to her and drove off at once, hiding her face so that they would not see the fear. They travelled without pause until evening and lay down and slept in the open, their white and yellow cloaks spread over them. When the boys slept, Fionnuala spoke to her; 'Promise me, Aoife', she said, 'that we will never return to the house of Lir'. And Aoife promised her.

The next morning it was not the song of thrush and blackbird that woke them but the shouts of men and the baying of hounds. Hearing them, Aoife rose immediately. She thought she might prolong their time if she crossed the water and confused the dogs. They were near Loch Dairbhreach, the Lake of the Oaks and it was there they fled.

The waters of the Loch were wide and dark blue, set in a bracelet of mountains. Seeing the cool, beautiful surface the youngest boys forgot their fear and stopped to bathe. Aoife drove the chariot through the shallow water until she emerged further down between two high trees. Fiachra and Conn left off their garments and entered the water and after a moment, seeing their joy, Fionnuala and Aodh followed. They played in the waters all four, careless and delighted as they had once been in their father's garden. And Aoife was the only one to hear the hounds draw near.

Conn the youngest came to the bank and turning

eyes upon her, clear and green as the fern that grew along the shore, asked:

'We will not go back, Aoife, will we? We will stay here free and wild as fish or birds always.'

'Yes,' Aoife answered him, fear beating up in her breast so that she could scarcely stand. In a few more minutes Lir would be upon them, they would be parted forever and still she could not fasten her resolve.

Taking Conn's hand she walked into the lake. She cursed herself because she had not the courage to do the only thing she could think of to save them. She stood trembling in the cold water, her hand on his shoulder. Then Fiachra came swimming towards her, arching his fine curving neck: 'Look, Aoife, what am I now?'

And seeing him she understood and knew what she must do. From under her cloak she took the druid rod and walking close to where they swam, touched with it first the head of Conn, then Fiachra, then Aodh and then Fionnuala until they were turned, the children, into four swans, white and strong and beautiful.

'It is with flocks of birds your cries will be heard now always', she called triumphantly. And they bent their smooth heads to her outstretched hands.

'You will keep your own voices and sing the sweet music of the fairies and your own sense and nobility will stay with you so that it will not weigh too heavy on you to be in the shape of birds,' and pushing them gently from her she said sorrowfully: 'Go away out of my sight now, with your stammering Irish, children of Aobh.'

And when Lir arrived with his dogs and horses and army he saw his wife standing alone in the rippled water and behind her on the shore the white and yellow cloaks of his children. And he was certain that she had murdered them.

He dragged her to his chariot and he and all his army set out for her father's kingdom.

And as he rode in fury from the lake he did not see the four white swans that sailed along the shore singing music of such beauty that even the dogs and the horses turned to listen. But Aoife heard and gazed back over her shoulder.

At her father's house she was brought before the court. They denounced her with terrible words.

'No punishment was fit', Lir said, 'for a woman who could murder children.' They called her a witch and a demon and the King declared that he would put her into that shape for all time so that no man would look at her face again.

But as the rod fell on her and they cursed her, a witch of the air, Aoife's soul gave thanks. For in that shape, though trapped in air, she could fly above the power of men to any place on earth her heart desired, far or near.

On the lakes and rivers of Ireland for many hundreds of years, four white swans sailed the clear waters singing music of such sweetness that women and men from all over the land came to hear it and every trouble and sickness they had was quieted by its beauty. And as they moved on the waters, the swans lifted their white heads and gazed into the air as if they beheld something unseen there that gave them protection and delight.

*Mary Dorcey*

# Ms Snow White Wins Case in High Court

In a landmark decision handed down in Court yesterday by Ms Justice Goodbye, Snow White was granted an injunction against seven men. MARK MIWORD reports on the case.

SNOW WHITE was yesterday granted an injunction in the High Court in Dublin, restraining a total of seven men from entering or interfering with the premises in the heart of the woods which had been shared between them for ten years. The Court heard how Ms White had been abused for a total of ten years by the defendants, since she was seven years old. In an *ex tempore* judgement, Ms Justice Goodbye said that it was the worst case she had ever been forced to hear.

At the conclusion of the hearing, which lasted four days, there was uproar from the seven defendants, who had to be carried forcibly from the body of the Court. Police were forced to arrest three of the defendants as they emerged, and all pleaded guilty to a breach of the peace in a special sitting of the District Court, and were fined £2 each and bound over.

Yesterday was devoted entirely to the judgement, as evidence had been taken earlier from both the plaintiff and defendants. In outlining the evidence which had been given, Justice Goodbye said that it was obvious that the defendants, by their own admission, had never made any attempt to offer compensation to Ms White, and that the worst aspect of the entire case was that they had shown no remorse for their actions over the years. In fact, the contrary was the case, as the defendants sought to justify their behaviour, and thereby compounded the wrong.

Justice Goodbye outlined the circumstances under which the case came before her. Ms White had been abandoned in the heart of the forest, when she was seven years old, by an agent acting on behalf of her stepmother, who wished to get rid of her. She pointed out, *inter alia*, that it was posssible to bring an action for cruelty on foot of this. Ms White, after wandering around for some considerable time, had then stumbled upon a small house. Exhausted, she had lain down to sleep. Upon awakening, she was confronted by seven men who were returning home from work as gold-diggers. Justice Goodbye made the point that Ms White was in no fit mental or physical condition, by virtue of her age and circumstances, to make any decision which could amount, under any circumstances, to 'the right to choose', in the legal sense of the word. Consequently, everything which took place following the initial encounter was tainted.

Messrs Dopey, Sneezy, Happy, Grumpy, Doc, Sleepy and Bashful proceeded to enter into a contract with Ms White, who was still exhausted, and in any event, of an age not legally held to be old enough to enter into a contract. Effectively under duress, Ms White agreed, following various promptings from the seven men, to look after the house while they were out gold-digging. She also agreed to cook and wash for all seven, to make the beds, to sew and knit and generally look after their welfare. Ms Justice Goodbye said that the contract,

apart from its earlier-mentioned failings, was further flawed in so far as there was no limit to the contractual obligations entered upon by Ms White. In return for agreeing to those conditions, Ms White was allowed to sleep in the house, and also to have enough food to eat. The contract, in the words of Justice Goodbye, was 'a travesty of natural justice'. She said also that Ms White must have been 'the handiest slave these seven men would ever have the good fortune to encounter'.

The seven men were so content with their lot that they took to singing songs upon their exit from the house each morning and upon their return in the evening. Ms Justice Goodbye outlined the duties which Ms White was expected to perform. She was forced to get up two hours before any of the seven men, and prepare their breakfast. At the same time, she had to gather wood to light the fire and ensure that the house was clean by the time the seven decided to get up. She herself did not get anything to eat until they left. On occasion, there was very little food left and she was forced to wait until dinner time before she ate properly.

With regard to the washing of their clothes, Justice Goodbye rehearsed the evidence that had been given, to the effect that the seven never took any care of themselves when they were out digging for gold. Knowing that they had someone at home to do 'all the dirty work', their behaviour was such as to suggest that they were deliberately creating work for Snow White. Ms White had given evidence of the filthy nature of all seven men. They left their clothes where they fell before they went to bed, and she was expected to cater to their smallest whim. This, said Justice Goodbye, was somewhat at odds with the claim of the defendants'

Counsel that all seven were self-styled New Age men in touch with the own feelings and emotions. Throughout all of this, the seven men continually reminded Snow White that on no account should she attempt to open the door during their absence. To this end, they warned her about all manner of dangers which she might face should she disobey them. Justice Goodbye pointed out that even though this 'warning' might well be grounded in a genuine concern for Ms White's 'welfare', the defendants had brought no evidence forward during the hearing to support their claim. The result of these 'warnings' was that Ms White lived in virtual isolation for many years, unaware that around the cottage a small township had grown up.

As Ms White reached maturity, it appeared to her that the seven men became more 'friendly', in her own words, and she believed that they were viewing her in a different light from hitherto. Gradually, it became clear that some of the seven had designs on her. Justice Goodbye pointed out that it was left to Ms White herself to make clear that 'conjugal rights' had been no part of the original contract. The Justice took the view that this was 'outlandish behaviour' on the part of some of the seven, and that 'it was an extension of the contract which no right-thinking person' would agree with.

The defendants, said Ms Justice Goodbye, had given evidence to the effect that throughout their careers as gold-diggers, they had made what they described as 'a fair bit of money'. However, none of this wealth had ever found its way to Ms White, nor indeed had gone any way towards making her life in the house any easier. The Justice said that the only conclusion that could be drawn was that the seven had hidden their wealth, and that they had no intention, even at this late stage, of making amends to Ms White. The Justice also pointed out that it was open to Ms White to enter a claim on the entire property in the woods, with a view to ensuring complete title to the entire estate. The Justice felt that 'any court in the land would surely look most favourably on any such claim'. Consequently, Justice Goodbye said that she had no hesitation in making an order restraining all seven defendants from entering or interfering with the house in the woods. Leave to appeal was refused.

After the disturbances, during which one of the defendants, Mr Grumpy, started to shout abuse at the Justice, Ms White appeared outside the Court with her close friend and supporter, Ms Rapunzel. Speaking to reporters, Ms White said that her life had been 'like a bad fairytale' for the past ten years.

Last night, a spokesperson for the Council for Civil Liberties said that they wished Ms White 'all the best for the future' but that the judgement itself held 'grim prospects' for other cases in that every person who thought they had a case similar to Ms White might now take an action, but that the action might fail, and thus 'hopes would be raised which might not be fulfilled'. The Council said that it was exploring the setting up of a working party to look at the implications of the case for gold-diggers. At some time in the future they may, or may not, publish a report.

*Clodagh Corcoran*

# Riding Hood

In my scarlet patched-together coat
I built a cage of teeth of rusty tin.
I fitted seven locks with ancient numbers -
forgot the numbers - clambered in.
My cloak had once been bitten from my body
by a wolf-grandmother, old and wild.
But I was never to speak of it.
I was only a child.
It was my secret with granny,
the only one who knew,
and the wood filled up with snarls
between us as I grew.
Now she prowls with eyes and ears
larger than she can use. She lingers.
She thrusts cold claws at me through bars;
they become warm fingers.
She wants to mend my riding hood
but I'm wrapped in it against her pleas;
I know a woman from a wolf
but I suspect apologies.
My hood and I are safer in my cage
whatever meanings she may bring.
A grandmother is not a wolf
but stories can be anything.

*Zoë Fairbairns*

# Snida

Once upon a time there lived a poor couple who owned a small huckster shop in a small midland town, in a small country, famous for tax concessions and race horses. Alas, the old couple found it very hard to make ends meet. All day long, it seemed, they were filling out forms, paying bills, and sending in tax returns. Although they sold Wellington boots and bush-saws, fishing tackle and bull's eyes, mats and chocolate bars, and they had a bar at the back of the shop that sold beer and spirits, their money seemed to run away like sand on a windy beach.

They had three daughters. The eldest was Jerravilda, called after a friend in the building trade. The second was Buttercup, called after a cousin in the city and the third was Snida, named after a rich foreign gentleman who had bought up fishing rights in the local lake.

They were very happy girls and they loved their father and mother very much. But nothing pleased them more than to run wild in the fields or to swim in the lake so that their mother would sigh as she mended and washed their clothes, 'They have me heart broke.' Their father, who worked night and day to keep the shop going and eventually shut the bar because he had only one customer, Lame Mick, on a Saturday night, would also sigh and say, 'Yez'd think they were wee lads, the things they get up to.' For the old couple had but one ambition; to get their three daughters a fine education.

As time went on and the children grew there were so many demands made on them for school books, blazers, gym tunics and white socks that the couple grew more and more depressed. One day the old man took the woman aside saying, 'I cannot go on any longer'. He turned to the wall and died.

Shortly after this the poor woman gathered her three daughters to her and in mournful tones declared that she, too, was worn out and that her time had come to join her husband. So the three girls wept bitterly as they closed their mother's eyes and laid the good woman in her coffin.

Jerravilda, who was now seventeen years old, had to look after her younger sisters and the shop as well. Every day she opened up at nine o'clock and when Ger and Peadar and Pink Patsy came for their quarter of sweets and when Ger's mother came in three minutes later, regular as clockwork, for the sliced pan, and Ger's father came in an hour and a half later for his twenty cigarettes, Jerravilda was always ready with a smile and the change and a 'It's not such a bad morning after all.' No-one in the town, and God knows the town was ready for gossip, could but say, 'Is that not the most polite wee girl that ever was?'

But Jerravilda had a problem. Apart from balancing the books, and filling out tax returns, ordering the stock and trying to persuade Lame Mick that the bar no longer existed, she was very beautiful.

She had long dark hair, jet black, that fell in folds right down to her waist. She tried to hide this by coiling it up and placing a dull comb firmly in the back of the mass. Her pale skin was without a blemish and her large kindly eyes were flecked with hazel like an autumn leaf. She had thick brows and a small happy mouth that had great difficulty in appearing severe. She had always been full of mischief, hanging out of other people's drain pipes and dare-devilling in the old quarry, stealing old boats and rowing out on Lough Guenah in the dead of the night, but now, alas, she had to put all that behind her.

She still attended the local secondary school and was about to sit her final examinations. Furthermore, she had to see that Buttercup kept herself neat and did her homework and that Snida could be got in from the fields and set to work in her second year at secondary school.

Buttercup was also beautiful, with eyes of a turquoise blue, wild hair, the colour of horse chestnuts, and she too loved to run in the wind and play will-o'-the-wisp with the other girls in the town (that is, when they were allowed out from their kitchens). But Snida was the real problem. When she wasn't kicking football in the hill field, she'd have her head stuck in a book. Jerravilda wouldn't have minded if Snida was reading a school book. But no. They were books on applied and quantitative mathematics, physics and interplanetary atmospherics, which had nothing whatever to do with the school curriculum.

Alas, Jerravilda grew so worried that she failed to get enough points in her final examination in order to go to third level education. While she worked and slaved and sent in the correct tax returns and prevented Lame Mick from jumping over the counter, she'd failed.

She was overcome with depression. For days and days she didn't go out of the shop. In spite of the fact that Buttercup and Snida said, 'Never mind, you have too much on your mind,' poor Jerravilda was frozen with misery. One day when she was looking at herself in the mirror she said to it, 'Mirror, Mirror, I'm not just a pretty face. I do have a brain. I do. I do.' But then she took out her results and read them over again and she burst into floods of tears.

Buttercup did all she could to cheer her up. 'What does an old exam matter? Sure we're all the same. You're as clever as everyone else. It's just that you have to do too much, look after the shop and mind us two and everything and go to school and study and who cares about all those silly marks anyway?' So Jerravilda dried her eyes and made Buttercup promise to work really hard so she'd be able to get all the As and Bs in the world and make all those so-and-so's in the town sit up.

So Buttercup looked in the mirror saying, 'Mirror, Mirror, please make me clever and not just a pretty face,' but the mirror just smiled back and didn't answer.

Every ragtag and bobtail in the town came looking for her. As soon as Jerravilda would shoo them out the front they were in the back. You see, not only was Buttercup beautiful, the local lads imagined that the shop was worth a fortune.

Alas, the three poor sisters hadn't a penny piece to their names. The bank owned the whole lot. Jerravilda tried not to think about it. But first thing in the morning and last thing at night she thought about it and all during the day she thought about it and she wondered, oh how she wondered, what was to become of them when the bank gave them no more credit and they had no roof over their heads.

Then one day a big black car drew up outside the shop and in walked a fine gentleman in a sheepskin coat, twill trousers, a yellow scarf and a trilby hat.

Jerravilda bid him a polite good morning and asked what he wanted. He said he was a film director and was looking for a hotel. Jerravilda told him the only hotel was up the street. But instead of thanking her and going away he lingered in the doorway, one foot in and one foot out. Then to her surprise he turned back in. He came right up to the counter and stared at her, without saying a word. Jerravilda smiled, wondering if there was something she could sell him, dusting and changing the packages behind the counter; the silent stare was making her nervous. After a moment or two he said, 'Do you own this shop?' 'I do,' she answered. 'I see,' he said and abruptly wandered off, letting the door bang behind him.

'Oh my God,' thought Jerravilda, immediately fearing the worst. 'He must really be a bank official. I'm finished now.' It was all too much for her and, for the second time that year, she burst into tears. Buttercup came running in, 'Oh, what is the matter, dearest Jerravilda?' 'The man from the bank,' sobbed Jerravilda, 'the man from the bank. He'll take everything. What will become of us?' The two sisters hugged each other and at eleven o'clock that evening they were still crying and hugging each other.

Next morning Jerravilda, having got both her sisters up, washed and off to school, was dusting the shelves and sweeping the floor when in walked the same gentleman, as suave as you please. 'Aha,' says he, 'the beautiful little shop-owner!' And flicking his cuffs down from under his sleeves, he continued, 'You have a handy piece of property here, I'd say. Right in the middle of town.'

Jerravilda's terror ran right down her back and into her shoes. 'You say you're a film-director?' she cried,

77

her voice barely audible. 'Oh yes, yes. I'm working on a cash film money spinner. Worth millions,' he said airily, extending a box of cigars, and when she shook her head, continued, 'and yes, I think this town would be just right for the location.'

Perhaps he's not from the bank after all, she thought. He is convincing. A tiny spark of optimism began to kindle in her heart. 'I must introduce myself,' he babbled on. 'My name is Prince O'Conmen, Ensign Films Incorporated.'

Jerravilda permitted herself a smile; bank spy or not at least it was a change from Ger and Pink Patsy and the quarters of mixed sweets. However, she still wasn't sure.

'What's the name of the film?' she ventured after a minute or two.

'It's er ... called ... *The* er... *White Feather*. All about the rebellion.'

'Which rebellion?' she persisted, determined to get to the bottom of it.

'The ninety-eight rebellion, of course, and ... er ... perhaps you'll tell me your name.'

'Jerravilda.'

'Charming, charming. Absolutely charming.' And that was the beginning of it.

Every day Prince O'Conmen visited the shop. He hung around asking all sorts of questions. During the second week he proposed marriage.

'But what about my sisters?' asked Jerravilda.

'Why, we can all live here together,' he said, looking at his watch as though he were timing her reply.

Now, although he reminded her sometimes of a fox that had recently broken covert, she had to admit that with his money her problems might be solved. At least her sisters would be able to get the fine education she craved for them.

Alas, poor girl, she was sadly taken in by all his boasting. When she told Buttercup and Snida of her plans, they threw themselves before her. 'Jerravilda, dearest Jerravilda, are you sure you want to marry Prince? You mustn't, oh you mustn't sacrifice yourself for us,' they chorused, and Snida added that when she grew up she would keep them all in luxury. 'How, dearest Snida, how?' the two eldest sisters asked, but Snida only smiled, saying quietly, 'You shall see.'

But Jerravilda had already decided to accept him, although underneath it all her heart was heavy.

The date was set and the two younger sisters mournfully accompanied her up the aisle.

The couple spent the honeymoon in the Isle of Man, Prince having paid for it with a strange-sounding credit card.

Time passed. Prince settled in. But there was no sign of the film crew. If Jerravilda asked him, 'When will they be coming?' he'd say, 'Anytime now,' handing her his shoes to polish or his jacket to brush. He was never satisfied. He insisted on the most expensive meals, new furnishings, fresh paint on the walls, and not only Jerravilda but Buttercup as well had to run around all day painting and putting up shelves, cooking and seeing to his personal needs. So when Buttercup went to sit her final examination she, too, failed miserably.

'Oh what, oh what will become of us?' Jerravilda cried. 'When I ask Prince for money, he says, "Not yet, not yet." When I ask him to help us in the house he says he has a bad back or a headache which can only be cured in the pub. And the till is empty every day. Oh, what will become of us all?'

At last it was Snida's turn to sit her exams and lo and behold, the little tomboy who liked nothing better than to run around in patched jeans not only got all As and Bs, she also won the County Scholarship. So she went off to college in the city.

Shortly afterwards another stranger came to the shop. He was even more splendidly dressed than Prince and drove up in a fine white sports car. He said he was Prince's brother Duke and claimed to be the owner of a multinational industry. He told them that, although Prince had not turned out as well as he hoped, he, Duke, would set them all on their feet again, adding, 'It's a very well-placed property you have here.'

Alas, with his soft talk and lying ways, he wooed and won Buttercup.

So the four of them settled down in the house behind the shop.

'He'll be as bad as Prince,' Jerravilda would say, but Butttercup would answer, 'No, no, dear Jerravilda, he really is rich. He says his money will come next week and then all our troubles will be over.'

But next week was soon next month, and then next year, while the two sisters got deeper and deeper in debt.

As soon as Snida arrived in college her tutors quite quickly realised that she knew just as much as, if not more than, they did, about differential calculus, numerical analysis, simulation theory, cybernetics and the theory of irrational numbers. And the boys in her year, well, the boys knew nothing at all on the subjects. In a very short time, it seemed, she was awarded a first class honours degree in Engineering and the following week she found herself solely in charge of building a bridge, not very far from her own home town.

Snida was overjoyed. Soon she would live at home again for, truth to tell, during these years of study she had missed her two sisters dreadfully.

The following week Snida came bounding into the shop, expecting her two sisters to be in fine clothes and the shop to be doing a flourishing trade. But when she saw them in old patched clothes and the cobwebs hanging off the walls of the rooms, a lump came into her throat. 'My darling Jerravilda, my darling Buttercup,' she cried, going down on her knees before them. 'How are you reduced to such misery? You have been brain-washed by those two warlocks.'

It was true. The two men had subtly cast a spell over the sisters. They had convinced them that they, and only they, were of any importance; that they remained smart and trim, their clothes washed and brushed as before, and that all the money in the till was to be used for their entertainment in the pub up the street.

Snida wrung her hands and clutched her brow. How, oh how could she break the dreadful spell that they were under?

'Tell you what,' she said, jumping to her feet, 'As soon as Prince and Duke have gone out, let you two put on your oldest jeans and come with me to the bridge. I'll find jobs for you. After all, I'm the boss of the outfit.'

By the time the two sisters had reached the bridge they had already begun to feel different. The air blew soft as swan's down on their cheeks and the sunbeams dancing on the stone melted the icicles in their hearts.

Day after day they went off to work, getting stronger and stronger all the time.

Prince and Duke were obliged to serve in the shop, if

they were to have any money at all. This they found very much beneath them.

When the sun had climbed to its meridian and the swallows had taught their young to fly, the knots that bound the girls to their husbands were completely severed. There only remained one problem. How to get rid of the lazy men!

'If we lock the till,' cried Snida, 'they'll have no money for themselves.' For the men had long ago sold their cars and relied on the few shillings the shop brought in. 'Then,' she added, 'perhaps they'll get on their bikes and pedal off.'

So the women took it in turns to mind the shop, taking care to see that the men got no money at all.

On the fifth month Prince turned to Duke and said, 'It strikes me, brother, we are not very popular around here any more.' And Duke turned to Prince and said, 'Brother, I agree with you. Perhaps it's time we packed our bags and sought our fortunes elsewhere.' So they did just that and took the bus to the city, giving their names and address to the driver, because they had no busfare.

When the sisters returned, tired, hungry and happy, and saw no sign of the brothers, at first they felt worried, then they felt guilty, and then, suddenly they felt little smiles dimpling their cheeks and laughter bubbling in their throats, and Snida bounced up and down like the little girl she really was at heart.

'It's all your doing, Snida, darling,' said Jerravilda.

'You're the sweetest, cleverest little girl in the world,' said Buttercup, and the two elder sisters hugged and kissed her while all three danced around the room.

And yes, as you may imagine, with the aid of Snida's salary, and the hard work of her sisters, in less time

than it takes to tell, the shop became the best in the town and the three sisters lived happily as happily could be.

*Leland Bardwell*

# The Frog Prince

ONCE UPON A time, in a far off land, there lived a king and queen with three beautiful daughters. The eldest, the auburn-haired Princess Marigold, decided, at the age of eighteen, that life at court was not for her and one night she slipped out of the palace, leaving a note on the hall table, and got the boat to England. She began travelling around the country with a well-known pop star. She was, in other words, a groupie. The Palace Press Officer explained her absence by saying that she was following a musical career abroad and, in a way, that's just what she was doing.

The second daughter, the blonde Princess Esmerelda, had also opted out and became involved with a religious sect. She was to be seen in the main shopping street of the capital stopping passers-by and trying to convert them. Luckily, she used an assumed name and, with her head shaved except for a long pony tail, some strange marks on her nose and a long blue robe, she was quite unrecognisable. The statement announced that Her Royal Highness had taken up missionary work.

The raven-haired Princess Matilda was the youngest daughter and she was by far the fairest. By the time she had come of age, the kingdom was in such a sorry state that the king had been forced to borrow enormous sums of money and now he was out of his tiny mind trying to think of ways to meet the interest payments. He was also worried that his subjects might begin to ask awkward questions if he allowed another daughter to fade into obscurity. After all, they had to have someone as a leader of fashion, didn't they?

Then, as the king sat in his jacuzzi one morning, a smile came over his face. Inspiration had hit him at last. He would marry Matilda off, just like they used to in the olden days. She'd object, naturally, at first, but she was a kind young woman and fond of her old dad. He thought he could talk her round - the promise of a crown jewel or two might help. They were only paste, but would she know? He closed his eyes and thought with pleasure of all the revenue a royal wedding would bring, TV and film rights, video sales, seats on the processional route, souvenirs, special flags and bunting. Just think of all the tourists who would come flooding into the country and, another thing, a distraction like this might get the workers off his back for a bit.

But who could he persuade to marry her and, more important, who could she be persuaded to marry? Princess Matilda was certainly attractive but unfortunately at her christening the Wicked Fairy had wished brains on her, a fate which hadn't befallen the princes in the neighbouring lands. Most of the good-looking princes were dim and busy trying to get into television. One, Prince Richard, had succeeded and was now to be seen reading the news, incognito, of course.

No, he'd have to look farther afield. Hold on, what about Prince Phillippe of Pieland? His family had money and might be willing to go halves with the wedding expenses.

Prince Phillippe was not a pretty sight, well below average height and beginning to run to fat. He already

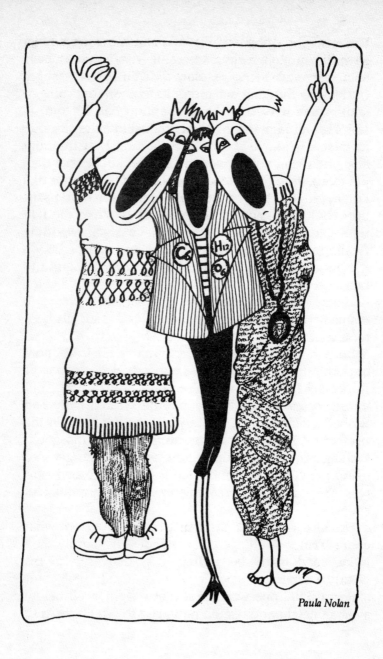

Paula Nolan

had a slight stoop and his extreme bow-leggedness gave him a most unusual walk. His large protruding eyes were a rather unpleasant muddy colour and his croaky voice and thick accent made him very hard to understand.

Try as he might, the king couldn't think of another candidate, so he approached Prince Phillippe's family to sound them out. Naturally, they were delighted with the suggestion. They had long ago given up hope of finding anyone short-sighted enough to want to marry their son. So eager were they that they offered to pay three-quarters of the wedding costs and Prince Phillippe seemed pleased with himself.

'So far, so good,' said the king to himself, 'now to persuade Matilda to marry Phillippe.'

'I hadn't really planned on getting married at all, Papa,' she began when he put his proposition to her. So he quickly brought up the subject of the crown jewels, hoping to tempt her, but Matilda was not to be won over with the promise of jewels.

'Oh come off it, Papa,' she laughed. 'As a child, I always suspected they were paste, so I did a chemical analysis on them to make sure.'

'Oh, those wretched brains of hers.' The king sighed and then realised his daughter was still speaking.

'Anyhow, that sort of stuff is considered pretty hick nowadays. I mean, how many people wear tiaras to a rave-up?'

The king scratched his head. That was a poser and no mistake.

'I give up,' he said at last.

'Oh, Papa, you really are a fool,' Matilda said, affectionately squeezing his arm.

'Thank you, my dear,' he said, trying to look modest.

'Look, Papa, I can see the mess you're in and I'd like to help. I feel rather sorry for this poor Phillippe person, I mean he looks so grotty, but I'll agree to marry him on one condition.'

'Anything , my love!' said the king eagerly.

'That you'll pay for my enrolment for an evening degree course in Science.'

The king was delighted and readily agreed. Prince Phillippe had no objections to his bride being busy four nights a week. After all, it would leave him free to follow local tradition and spend his evenings in the pub with the other husbands.

The wedding was arranged for September so that the princess could be back from the honeymoon in time for the start of the academic year.

I won't bore you with the details of the wedding; weddings are much the same the world over. I will just tell you that Princess Matilda looked beautiful and that the sun shone and the media paid over large sums of money to bring the spectacle to the viewing public.

Thanks to Prince Phillippe's family contribution there was plenty to eat and drink and then, after a decent interval, the happy couple retired to the bridal suite, as happy couples are wont to do.

The next morning, at eight o'clock, there was a tap on the door of the royal bedchamber and in came a palace maid-servant with the early morning tea. She was more than surprised to find Princess Matilda alone.

'Er, excuse me, your Royal Highness,' the maid-servant began, putting the tray down on the bedside table, 'but ...'

'Oh, it's quite all right. Don't look so worried. His Highness is in the bath. Come and see,' she said, and jumping out of bed, she took the startled girl's hand

and pulled her, protesting, into the bathroom. And there in the bath was the most beautiful frog you have ever seen.

'Isn't it wonderful?' Princess Matilda looked radiant. 'You see, Zoology is my favourite subject. I'm planning to write a paper on animal behaviour and now I have my very own frog. I wonder if a frog could be trained to retrieve balls from wells?' she mused to herself.

Then she smiled dreamily, knowing that she, at least, was going to live happily ever after.

*Anne Cooper*

# That'll Teach Her

ONCE UPON A time there was a storybook called *Grim Words for Children*. It was coloured green and red and belonged to a seven-year-old girl called Maoliosa. Maoliosa lived at the end of a long lane. She could see the wood from her bedroom window, but not always the trees, if, for instance, there was a fog. She was friendly with the wood and the trees and all the elements including the wind. Maoliosa was an only child and depended largely on her books for friendship. She got on particularly well with *Grim Words for Children*, perhaps because she didn't know what 'grim' meant. Before the time when she herself could read, her mother, who was the most wonderful woman imaginable, used to read to her. Her mother lived with Maoliosa's stepfather. Actually he wasn't really her stepfather because her mother wouldn't marry him due to the fact that she didn't believe in marriage. However, he was the nearest thing to a stepfather that Maoliosa would ever have. One thing that always worried Maoliosa was that she didn't like one story in the book, but she never thought that she could say it for fear of upsetting her mother. This story was called *The Little Red Shoes* or *That'll Teach Her*. So when Maoliosa could read herself she always skipped this story. The other stories felt fine, although occasionally some of them appeared a little bloated because of over-confidence or a little restricted because of over-moralism.

One night Maoliosa accidentally started to read *The Little Red Shoes*. She read the first two lines and tried to stop when she realized her mistake, but she couldn't. The book had stuck to her hands, the words had grabbed on to her eyes like plungers and she could not stop reading. She read and read, late into the night, the horrible tale of the poor little girl who wanted to dance and who consequently ended up footless, degraded and a skivvy to a priest. When she had finished the story tears were rolling down her cheeks. She had to cry for hours and hours before the cumulative effect of the wet tears could unseal her eyes from the dreadful story. She fell asleep chastened, terrified and lonely and she dreamt frighteningly all night. She dreamt of a world where cruelty abounded. Priests and other men ruled this world and would not let any women talk to each other. If there was a gathering of two women or more it was outlawed on the grounds that the women could pass on subversive information to each other. Young women were reared for competitions and older women were thrown out when their masters decided that they were finished. Maoliosa dreamt of blind women who were fooled by everyone because they couldn't see, grey-haired women who were scorned, and young girls who were battered, melted down and manipulated into whatever shape their masters wanted. She woke, very sad, but relieved to know that life wasn't quite that awful. Maoliosa vowed never to open the book again.

Time passed. Maoliosa continued to read other books but often missed *Grim Stories for Children*. Sometimes as she lay in bed at night she worried about the story. Could it be possible that enjoying yourself was intrinsically evil? Could it be possible that all joy, all spontaneous expression, would lead to dismemberment? Could it be possible that there was only one way to mourn your mother, in black? She remembered the time that Missus Kelly had turned up at her husband's funeral in a purple leather coat. Everyone had said things like, 'Ah now, she *never* had much sense.' 'Did you *ever*?' 'Not much good *ever* came from that parish,' or 'poor Mister Kelly'.

So it was true. *The Little Red Shoes* was true. She would stop playing and try to push to the back of her mind the fact that she wanted to be a dancer when she grew up. She couldn't afford to think about the shoes part at all, at all, because in fact she just loved red shoes. Oh dear. What a problem for troubled little Maoliosa. She was nearly as badly off as the poor little girl in the story. Of course she still had her feet but that was only because she had not yet worn red shoes, nor had she started to dance.

One day when she was tidying her room she unintentionally moved *Grim Stories for Children* from her shelf to the large brown dressing table that had mirrors looming everywhere, out into the room, into each other and straight down into the wood. She left it there overnight and as she slept a strange thing happened. A light wind started to blow at the bottom of the wood. It whistled softly to itself, rocking the trees gently, then moved up through the wood, gathering momentum as it reached Maoliosa's window. It blew and blew on the window until it opened the cover of *Grim Stories for Children*. Maoliosa turned sleepily in her bed and pulled the clothes up around her ears to keep the cold out. The wind blew

92

*Kate White*

and blew until each of the pages of the book turned themselves and faced the mirror. At last page one of *The Little Red Shoes* faced its own reflection. The wind stopped and settled itself down outside the house, leaning against the gable wall, to see if what she had planned would materialise. The story looked at itself, first rather reluctantly, then more brazenly. It began to read itself and although it cringed a little it continued, drawing on its reserves of cocksuredness in order to finish the first page. It turned the next page itself, not particularly worried, but when it came to page three it just couldn't continue. The wind kept up its insistence until eventually *The Little Red Shoes* had completely read itself. The book collapsed in a heap on the dressing table and wept bitterly. The wind apologised for any pain that it had caused but whispered, 'I really cannot see how I could have avoided any longer doing what I did.' It then withdrew to the bottom of the wood and slept a satisfied sleep.

The following week was a busy one for *The Little Red Shoes*. The more it thought, the more uncomfortable it felt. It was indeed more than a little shaken by its own profile but then it would try not to think because after all, what could it do? It had always been this way. How could it change? I mean, really change. Where would it all end if it even tried to reform a little? Some of the other stories began to complain because they weren't being read and what was the point in being a story if you weren't being read? Other stories were downright rude to *The Little Red Shoes* and yet more were conciliatory but emphatic that something had to be done. Some didn't care one way or the other, while the rest said that they were all stories in the end and that if they didn't pull together where would they end up? Not in books certainly, out on the road more likely, blown there by the wind of ill fortune. But gradually *The Little Red Shoes* itself decided to change a little. First it changed in small ways when no-one was looking, dropped an odd word, changed the occasional sentence around, added bits and pieces here and there. But then it felt badly patchworked, some parts just did not fit with others so it decided one night, 'Fuck this, I'm going to have to go the whole hog.' And it did. In what must be said was an extremely brave swoop it did a complete job on itself, turning inside-out and upside-down to make a completely different story. It was interesting really because when it consulted its individual parts they were all delighted to change. The shoes said they were exhausted always dancing, and that it wasn't much fun leading the girl into such terrible trouble. The old woman said that she herself liked to dance and didn't mind the colour red. The woman who was living with the parson said that she didn't necessarily believe in cheap labour. Best of all, the executioner said that he hadn't believed in capital punishment for some time. And the little girl explained quite logically that like Emma Goldman she didn't want to be part of any story if she couldn't dance. *The Little Red Shoes* began to feel wonderful.

But it didn't end there. After some time the other stories began to question their complacency. They were a little envious of the new *Little Red Shoes* so they began some shuffling about. The ugly duckling refused to run away and soon the other ducks had to undergo some re-evaluation of the meaning of beauty. Pandora was complimented for her natural good sense in facing reality and Epimetheus was scorned for being such a sleeveen. You want to see what some of the others decided! Then they all went to a party in the wood with the wind and next morning they woke under Maoliosa's pillow. She smiled and decided to give the book one more try.

*Evelyn Conlon*

# Happy Ever After and Other Obsessions

ONCE UPON A time there was a little girl who was born with a head of thick fair hair. It seemed at the time to be the only propitious circumstance around, for giant question marks stood over her future. One morning however, a tall dark woman in black spotted her in her orphanage cot, and brought her home to a Martello tower in the country. We are going to live happily ever after, she crooned.

Nobody quite knew how she squared it with the adoption workers, and people in the village talked, as people do. Some said the dark woman was really the child's grandmother; others said there must be some nasty secret lurking in that old tower. One old man said that the herbs she grew on the balcony were poisonous. The dark woman would never let anyone past the front door. She spent a lot of time in the round room at the top of the tower painting, and little Rapunzel, for that was the child's name, would paint too. The woman taught Rapunzel that the modern world was corrupt and full of danger, and that they were lucky to live so happily in the country. Television was an instrument of the devil, so Rapunzel was protected from its pernicious influence. Being a contented little girl she made her own amusements. The only difficulty was that she could never see any of the corruption her mother spoke of. At school, the teacher took her under her wing and she soon had lots of friends in the village.

Once the teacher had sent a note home suggesting that Rapunzel's hair should be cut. Rapunzel's mother flew into a rage. She said hair was a woman's crowning glory, that cutting it was unnatural. After that the teacher sent no more notes. Rapunzel's plaits grew so long they had to be looped up behind. She became adept at filtering school news so that it would not upset her mother, and home news so that it wouldn't upset the teacher. In this way she moved up through national school taking part in games and pantomimes. She dispensed her mother's herbs and was loved by everyone for her good nature.

When Rapunzel was about twelve, her mother gave up painting and became obsessed with food. Evil persons, she told Rapunzel, were trying to poison the world with additives and preservatives. She decided they would grow their own food. The nearest available land was two miles away, so each morning she would cycle off on an ancient bicycle, her black skirts billowing. At first Rapunzel came along to help, but the language of the neighbouring farmer was so coarse that her mother enjoined her to stay at home. By the time the girl was sixteen, her mother had also become suspicious of the education system, and Rapunzel did her lessons by correspondence. Even then some of the prescribed texts caused problems. Yet, in spite of all, Rapunzel retained her good humour.

Unfortunately, she was also beautiful, and her mother's next virulent obsession concerned men. Men, she told the wide-eyed Rapunzel, were the source of all evil, the reason why women did not live happily ever after. When she found her daughter conversing with a neighbour who happened to be male, tall and handsome, Rapunzel's days of freedom ended. She was moved up to her mother's old studio at the top of the tower. Rapunzel's mother was not cruel; the organic vegetable business was doing quite well (in spite of her being choosy about customers), and she installed a rose bathroom and a cooker. When the workmen were finished she blocked the stairs herself, so that the only entrance was from the wooden balcony. Rapunzel fought long and hard to have at least a fire escape but her mother was adamant. A way out is also a way in, she said. In the evening Rapunzel was to let her plaits down over a winch to allow her mother to visit.

At first even Rapunzel's sweet nature was not proof against this trial, and she just sat there not even eating the good organic vegetables. But gradually she recovered and thought of stratagems to make life bearable. Her old teacher smuggled her in books; one friend brought her a rope-ladder so she was occasionally able to escape to the village. Some people talked of informing the police, but they were afraid of the dark woman who was now openly referred to as the witch. Anyway Rapunzel was hopeful of her mother's latest obsession which concerned the seepage of radon gas. With any luck, Rapunzel thought, we'll remove to a cedarwood bungalow, and all this manoeuvring will be unnecessary. She cut off a foot of her hair and found that her mother didn't notice. Things were definitely looking up.

Then one day Fate came knocking on Rapunzel's tower in the shape of a youngish man in a stylish car. Rapunzel came out on the balcony with a copy of *Romeo and Juliet* in her hand. She thought the man below could make a passable stab at the part of Romeo.

Kate White

99

Another girl might have found him slightly stooped and lacking in hair, but Rapunzel had had enough of hair. Even with judicious snipping she still had several pounds of the stuff hanging around her and there were her mother's dark wisps as well. The man had kind eyes, she thought, and his obsession wasn't of the visible variety. He seemed a better prospect for happy ever afterhood.

He told her he was a lecturer doing a study of Martello towers and hers was the most interesting one he had seen to date. Could he come up and view it more closely?

'The entry arrangements are a bit weird,' she said. 'Can you climb hair?'

When she let down her yellow plaits, he fell on them and kissed them passionately (which should have warned her), then scrambled up.

Once there, he proved interesting. Rapunzel's head whirred with the things he told her and it was all she could do to expel him before her mother came back from planting her unadulterated onions. She was breathing her usual fire and brimstone, averring that men, particularly organic vegetable sellers, were only after One Thing. Rapunzel found no evidence of this in her relationship with Martin, for such was the young man's name. He was, it is true, fascinated by her hair, and liked to sit surrounded by yards of fuzz.

Rapunzel found this rather tiresome but put up with it for the secondary delights of his visits. One day she told him about her secret ladder, and suggested she meet him in the village that evening. Martin was unenthusiastic. He much preferred coming to the tower. It was an oasis of quiet in a mad world, he said. As they sat, arms entwined, under Rapunzel's sheltering hair, he told her of the problems of academia, the poisoned chalices, the illiterate students. Finally when Rapunzel, who had been reared on fairy stories, was becoming a bit impatient, he asked her to marry him.

'It would be nice to live here,' he said. 'But there's your mother.'

'And the lack of stairs,' Rapunzel added.

He said he would build a miniature tower for her in the city, but in the meantime happy ever after would mean a flat. Rapunzel heaved a sigh of relief and they decided to elope that very night.

That evening her mother seemed slower than ever at climbing the hair. Rapunzel felt guilty about leaving but could not conceal her impatience.

'Oh, hurry up, mother,' she called. But as soon as her mother stood beside her, Rapunzel knew that she knew. Maybe it was telepathy, maybe it was detective work, or maybe she really was a witch.

'You've had a man up here,' her mother spat, and whipping a knife from under her skirt, she sawed off Rapunzel's hair. 'I must protect you until you are able to recognise true happiness,' she said. When she descended she pulled Rapunzel's plaits down after her. Thank heavens she didn't find the rope ladder, Rapunzel thought. I'll just fix my hair and get going.

Rapunzel got to work with her nail scissors and by the time she left the tower, she had as little hair as Martin himself. He turned pale when she walked into the village pub.

'My God, girl, where is your lovely hair?' he said, his eyes filling with tears.

Rapunzel looked at him for a long moment.

'You mean you only loved me for my hair,' she said.

He turned away and she saw happy ever afterhood going as well.

'I could grow it again,' she offered in sacrificial tones, but just at that moment a dark figure appeared, laughing horribly, and threw something into Martin's face. He screamed and Rapunzel ran back to him.

'Slut! harlot!' her mother was shouting. 'You will never live happily ever after!' and she lashed the two of them with Rapunzel's plaits.

Well, it was the most exciting night the village had seen in a long time. Rapunzel's mother was carted off to the asylum, where the quality of the vegetables improved considerably. Poor Martin was rushed to hospital with eye damage. Rapunzel sat beside him in the ambulance and he confessed that he was a hair fetishist. She told him it didn't matter; she was into doing good herself and he could have her hair if he needed it.

Rapunzel stayed in the village and dallied with the handsome young neighbour. Then she dallied with the idea of Martin as a smouldering disabled husband *a la* Mr Rochester. She sought him out in the psychotherapist's clinic where he had gone to find himself. The psychotherapist was very interested in Rapunzel, and felt that with her equable nature and her experience of obsessions, she could have a bright future in psychotherapy. Rapunzel rose rapidly in the world of couches and non-direction, while Martin exorcised his experiences with a best-seller called *Hair and Punishment*. The two lived happily together on a provisional basis, with Rapunzel's plaits in a box under the bed.

*Máiríde Woods*

# The King, The Queen and The Donkey Man

ONCE UPON A time, the king and queen of the fairies made their home in a forest near the city of Athens in Greece. The king was named Oberon, and the queen, Titania; and both were very fond of doing what they pleased. Titania passed her days among the courtiers, a charming crowd of dainty fairies, who danced, told stories and tended the flowers that grew in the forest. Oberon, who regarded such pastimes as unmanly, escaped whenever he could with his pal, Puck, a renegade fairy and master prankster. Together, in the darkest leafy glades of the forest, Oberon and his sidekick would knock back quantities of fermented berry juice, and exchange wisecracks, which kept them amused for hours.

In the evenings, Oberon fluttered home, where the little fairies stuffed him full of blackberries, figs, and the honey bags from bumble-bees. Later, Titania massaged Oberon's back, while briefing him on the latest news of their fairy kingdom. As he drifted off to sleep, Oberon marvelled at how well this lifestyle suited him.

Indeed, things were going along swimmingly until the day that Titania was made guardian to a bouncing boy-child. Baby William was a lively human infant, with pink cheeks and yellow hair, and as different from the insubstantial fairies as chalk is from cheese. The

103

queen was devoted to him; and Oberon watched jealously as Titania played peepbo with the boy, and sang to him ancient fairy songs.

The fact was that Oberon desired the child for himself. He wanted the boy to walk in his own footsteps. He yearned to teach William all he knew: how to hunt for plover or squirrels in the forest; how to steal the finest feathers from a peacock; how to carve spears out of the best white oak. So, Oberon approached his queen with the confident, cocksure step of a king who generally gets his own way.

'The child is mine,' Oberon purred.

Titania stared him down with steely eyes. 'No way!' she said, folding her glittering wings around William.

Oberon was taken aback. 'I said, give me the boy,' he insisted, astonished to hear a titter from one of the fairy courtiers, who were all listening goggle-eyed.

'Over my dead body,' Titania smiled, and blew a kiss across the distance between them, much as if she were tossing in bandages after a hand grenade.

Shouting for Puck, the fairy king slouched off, his handsome face livid, and his mind dwelling upon revenge.

As it happened, there was a group of Athenian workers rehearsing a play in the forest. These workers were the salt of the earth, a carpenter, a cobbler, a miller, a weaver, and a tailor, all hard-working men who earned their bread through the use of their hands and the sweat of their brows. They were determined to make a success of their little play, even though they were unaccustomed to using big words and enacting strong emotions.

As Oberon and Puck flew through the forest, they chanced upon this rehearsal. Being quite invisible themselves, they decided to watch. In no time at all, they were roaring with laughter at the simple antics of the unsophisticated players.

'Who is that oaf playing the leading man?' Oberon inquired.

'He is Bottom, the weaver,' replied Puck.

'Then he's aptly named, for he is, indeed, the bottom of the heap!' Both the fairy king and his sidekick howled raucously, as if this witticism were very funny indeed.

His spirits revived, Oberon settled upon a plan to put Titania in her place. 'Why not make the fairy queen fall in love with this baboon, Bottom?' he murmured in a silky voice.

'Hah!' snorted Puck, 'That would be revenge indeed. Only, who could fall in love with such a bumpkin?'

'Look,' whispered Oberon. From the fob pocket in his waistcoat, the fairy king withdrew a tiny vial. 'Love-in-idleness! The juice of a pansy flower, impaled by Cupid's arrow. One drop on Titania's sleeping eyelids, and she will dote madly upon the next creature she sees.'

'Brilliant!' Puck was aquiver with excitement. 'But may I suggest a refinement?'

'By all means.'

'Give Bottom the head of a donkey, so then your queen might truly love an ass!'

'How perfectly vile!' Oberon agreed.

And so it came to pass that when Titania woke from her sleep, she fell madly in love with the weaver, Bottom, who had the body of a man, but the head of a donkey.

The spectacle of the lovely fairy queen in the arms of a donkey-man caused Oberon to slap his thigh with joy. 'Just listen to him talk,' Oberon sneered. 'He brays!'

Titania was too much in love to care. And Bottom was in love with Titania. In the evenings, the donkey-man sprinkled buds of musk-roses on to her bed, and wove violets into her golden hair. In the mornings, he made himself useful about the palace, weaving, market gardening, and playing on the pipes, so that the fairy courtiers might have music for their dancing. He was also good with Baby William. Together, the fairy queen and her lover played chase with the child, and Bottom was always ready to soothe away tears with a gentle nuzzle, or even to change a nappy, when the need arose.

Soon Oberon got bored with the sight of his mistress canoodling with a donkey, so he applied the antidote to Titania's eyes. He stepped back to enjoy the fun. With relish, he anticipated Titania's shriek at the sight of her lover's bristles and snout.

But it never came. The fairy queen failed to leap for protection into Oberon's waiting arms. On the contrary, she studied Bottom's rough features closely, and saw that they were shining with the goodness of his soul. The fact is that the donkey-man's kindness had made such an impression upon Titania's heart, that she loved him truly, no matter what he looked like.

Of course the restoration of her senses also made Titania understand the game that Oberon had been playing.

'What a nasty mocking mind you have,' she complained. 'Only a louse could cook up a scheme like that!'

'Now, now,' Oberon said sheepishly.

'Just keep your silly mouth shut,' Titania said. 'There

are some things you shouldn't mock, and love is one of them.'

So, with no more ado, Titania told Oberon to pack his bags and leave the forest. And that is what he did. Then Titania, the queen of the fairies, lived happily ever after with her new partner, Bottom, and the bouncing boy-child, William.

*Ivy Bannister*

Denise Kierans

# The Twelve Dancing Princesses

The blood tree sheds
its rubies, its molten golds,
groans when his blind weight
snaps a branch
As I go down the slow
spirals his foot treads
on my heels; step by step
he withholds me. Even the ferry
is stern down under
his great cloak. We may not
reach the island.

I cannot drowse him
into heedlessness. Old voices
in the wildwood warn him
of my spiced cup.

How his crotch sags, rogue
bull, old soldier; he
and my father are in league.
He has a kingdom to inherit,
and will dog me
until my slippers are spotless,
until my nights dance no longer.

*Roz Cowman*

Kate White

# The Frog Prince Revisited

PRINCE Frederick sat on a lily-pad at the edge of the pond and croaked mournfuly. It had all been a terrible misunderstanding. He had intended the remark that led him to the lily pond as a compliment to the new serving maid. How could he have known that she was a witch who would take offence and turn him into a frog? Sexist remark indeed! The trouble with women nowadays was that they had no sense of humour. It was lucky for him that his faithful partner, Henry, had seen what happened and rescued the frog prince. Henry had been just in time to save his master from becoming a squashed frog beneath the foot of a stoutly-shod scullion.

'It's all right,' Henry had assured Frederick, who had not yet recovered from the instant loss of six feet from his six-foot-three-inch height. 'I've read this story and I know the rules. You'll be a handsome prince again in no time at all as long as you do what I tell you.'

Henry had taken Frederick to a neighbouring kingdom and laid him gently on a lily-pad in a pond near the royal palace. Frederick had listened somewhat dubiously to the story Henry told him. Henry was a well-meaning but somewhat dim faithful retainer and Frederick was sceptical of the outcome of his scheme.

'How can I be sure that a princess will find me and release me from this spell?' he asked Henry.

'The royal family lives in the palace near here, 'said Henry. 'There are two princesses in the family and they're sure to come here to play.'

'And one of them will drop a golden ball in the pond and I have to rescue it for her,' said Frederick. 'Suppose she decides to pick it up for herself?'

'She'll never do that,' Henry assured the unhappy prince. 'Princesses are far too helpless and weak. She'll simply sit down by the edge of the pond and weep for the loss of her toy. That's where you come in.'

'At my size I doubt whether I could lift a cotton-wool ball, never mind a golden one,' Frederick said sadly.

'Don't be defeatist,' said Henry. 'Of course you can do it. It's in the story. All you have to do then is persuade her to take you home, allow you to eat off her plate, sleep in her bed with her and kiss you. Then, hey presto, you're a man again and ready to marry a princess and live happily ever after.'

'That should be easy enough,' Prince Frederick said vainly. 'Few girls can resist my charms, except for that witch, of course.'

'But,' said Henry, 'no girl would kiss you while you're under your present appearance. They don't like anything slimy, you know. They're very squeamish. You'll have to bargain with her. Don't give her back her golden ball until she's promised to take you home with her.'

'Isn't that blackmail?' Frederick asked.

'Stop making problems,' said Henry. 'Anyone would think you liked being a frog. Just do as I tell you and I'll come by over the next few days to see how you're getting on.'

'Henry, don't leave me,' pleaded Frederick in panic. 'I can't swim.'

But Henry was already out of earshot and Frederick was surprised to find out that he could swim. That had been ten days ago, though, and so far Frederick hadn't seen another person besides the faithful Henry. He came to the pond every day to see how Frederick was adapting to his new life. Frederick wasn't enjoying life as an amphibian. He had never realised that a lily-pond could be so fraught with danger.

'Only yesterday I had a very narrow escape from a stork,' he complained. 'Oh, please take me home. I haven't seen any sign of a princess here. At least I might be able to persuade that witch to reverse her spell at home.'

'Be patient,' Henry urged him. 'It will work out, you'll see. You'll be grateful when you've married a princess.'

So Frederick learned to avoid storks and to croak like other frogs.

At last the day came when he saw a party of young women approaching the pond. But his heart sank as they drew near enough for him to discern their features. They were common, rough-looking girls, not at all the delicate creatures he expected to be in the company of a princess. Instead of daintily tossing a golden ball around, they formed teams and began to play five-a-side soccer. Frederick wished they would go away and leave the area free for the princess. He felt a bit uneasy about the big, heavy-looking ball too. Suppose it should land on him. Frederick turned from emerald to pale green as one of the girls kicked it in the direction of the water and it hurtled towards the lily-pad where he was sitting. He leaped in the nick of time and landed on the ball just as it splashed into the water. A tall girl with short reddish hair and freckles

Catherine McConville

lifted both frog and ball out of the water. When she noticed the trembling frog, the girl exclaimed in surprise: 'It's a frog. It's just what I need for my collection of indigenous amphibia.'

Frederick opened his mouth and croaked weakly. He was still in shock and he hoped he had not lost his power of human speech.

'I hope he won't eat any of the other creatures, your highness,' another girl said. Frederick did not know whether he was more indignant at the suggestion that he would cannibalise the indigenous amphibia or surprised that this unlikely-looking girl was the princess he had been waiting for, Princess Freda. Somehow, he didn't think Henry had envisaged such a development.

'Excuse me, your highness,' Frederick croaked as loudly as he could, 'but I'd be much happier if you were to let me eat from your plate and sleep in your bed than I would be with the indigenous amphibia.'

'It talks!' exclaimed Princess Freda. 'This is most extraordinary. I'll have to take it to an amphibiologist. It must be a very rare species. It may not be indigenous at all.'

'Please,' said Frederick, paling as he remembered school biology classes and the unspeakable atrocities committed on frogs in the name of science. 'Just take me home and let me share your food and your bed.'

'I suppose it wouldn't do any harm,' said Princess Freda indulgently. 'He seems quite intelligent. I might even keep him as a pet.'

Frederick couldn't believe how easy it had been. What a fool Henry was! The girl was obviously quite bright, as girls go, and she knew he was no ordinary frog. That was why she hadn't been afraid to touch him. Of course she was a little tomboyish, but she'd soon change once she discovered his true identity. Once they were married, she'd look after him and keep house for him and cook for him and be there with his slippers ready by the fire when he came back from playing polo and other princely pursuits. Prince

Frederick sighed with contentment. He'd think of a suitable reward for Henry.

Princess Freda's infatuation with the frog met with amused tolerance from most of the royal family. Her elder sister objected to his presence at table saying it was unhygienic. Frederick thought of how surprised she would be when he had resumed his rightful shape. He sat complacently on the edge of Princess Freda's plate and munched his way through any titbits she proffered to him. It was good to eat food fit for a prince again. That evening, Princess Freda carried him to her room and laid him gently on the pillow beside her. One more night to go in this hideous frog's body and tomorrow ... Prince Frederick could hardly wait.

Prince Frederick and faithful Henry walked dejectedly through the gates of the palace where Frederick's family lived. They had barely escaped with their lives from the neighbouring kingdom.

'I don't understand,' Henry shook his head. 'You can't have followed my instructions. Tell me what happened again.'

'I did everything you told me,' Frederick protested. 'It was much easier than I expected it to be. She was delighted with me, especially when she found out that I could talk. Everything went perfectly. She took me home, she fed me from her plate, she even took me to bed with her. Then in the morning when she found me beside her she said,"Good morning, little frog" and kissed me. You know what happened then. All hell broke loose. Of course it was good to be human again, but we'd forgotten all about clothes, Henry. How could you have been so thoughtless? There I was, stark naked in Princess Freda's bedroom. She was no help. Before I could say a word, her expression changed from one of endearment to one of disgust. "Ugh, it's a man!" she yelled. I smiled feebly and said "Yes, and now that I'm my true shape, we can get married and live happily ever after." "Get married!" she was madder than ever at the suggestion. "How dare you? I'm fifteen years old and it will be at least ten years before I even consider getting married, if even then. You've wormed your way into my affections, shared my food, my bed ... it's outrageous! Get out of here." Then she began to throw things at me. I turned and ran out of the room as fast as I could. Of course, as soon as the palace guards saw a naked man running from Princess Freda's room they suspected the worst. I was captured and brought before the king and queen. Things looked ugly for a while. The queen recognised me as "that wastrel Frederick from next door". The king wanted to execute me on the spot, then declare war on us. Only for the fact that the queen and my mother are distant cousins, I don't know what would have happened. Of course, they wouldn't believe that I was the frog. "You must take us all for fools," the king raged. "I gave up believing in fairy tales when I was six." I was shivering as I still had nothing to wear. Fortunately, Princess Freda, who had come to tell her side of the story, took pity on me and had one of the servants find me some old clothes.'

'That was when I arrived on the scene,' said Henry. 'The guards were scouring the grounds looking for more intruders when I arrived at the pond. They picked me up as a suspicious character and one of Princess Freda's ladies-in-waiting said I'd been hanging around the pond for days.'

'Served you right,' Frederick said. 'It was all your fault in the first place. You and your stupid tales.'

116

'I did my best,' objected Henry. 'Anyway, you're human again. Surely that means something to you.'

'I'll be the laughing stock in two kingdoms,' said Frederick. 'I can't show my face in polite society again. Princess Freda wasn't a bad sort after all.' He sounded more than a little regretful. 'She verified my story. The king wouldn't believe me and neither would the queen. They thought Princess Freda had been the victim of a confidence trick but because of her, they decided to let me leave on condition that I never show my face, or any other part of me, in the kingdom again.'

'At least you were free to go,' said Henry. 'You weren't thrown into a dungeon and forced to eat bread and drink water. They wouldn't have released me if I hadn't been trying to talk to a frog that I thought might have been you; they thought I was a harmless lunatic.'

'A fitting end to the story,' Frederick said bitterly. 'I had time to explain how I came to be a frog to Princess Freda before I left. She laughed herself silly and told me she hoped I'd learned not to treat women as sex objects. Too true! I was afraid even to kiss her goodbye in case I turned into a frog again.'

Frederick and his faithful retainer Henry never said a word to anyone about the frog episode. News of it was hushed up in the other kingdom to save the princess embarrassment but she just thought it was a huge joke anyway. Life returned to what it had been - but Frederick never again passed sexist remarks. He stopped leading a life of pleasure and became a respected authority on pond life. No-one ever knew where Frederick obtained such interesting information on the life of frogs, except of course, for the princess, but she kept the secret.

*Anne Claffey*

# The Budgeen

ONCE UPON A time a long time ago there was a country whose customs were very different from ours. For a start everyone wore veils, men and women, so that none of their faces could be seen, and they were very frightened. They did not know what they were frightened of, because it was not the custom to ask. And they were very happy at being afraid. They would spend a lot of time chattering to one another, about how frightened they were and how everyone was afraid: 'God love her', they would say, 'she wouldn't say *boo* to a goose'. And the highest praise was, 'She's frightened of her own shadow'. And, of the men, who were always silent and would stand together at the street-corners looking like clumps of faded nettles, the women as they passed would simper coyly, 'The cat's got their tongues', and would giggle. From morning till night these women tittered, sipped, and skipped.

Except for one little girl called Macha, and she was too busy wondering why she was supposed to be frightened and what she was supposed to be frightened of to be frightened. Why could she not see anyone's face? Why could no-one see *her* face? What was the secret? One day, straight out without fear, she said to her father: 'Why is your face covered? I want to see your face.' Her father seized her and began beating her without giving her an answer. She fought back and her hand grabbed hold of his veil and all of sudden it came away from his face. What was worse, his nose fell off. And there he stood, without a nose.

Her mother cried out, 'What are we going to do?' You have ruined us! Your sisters and I will die of shame!' And, as was only proper, they did.

The father, who looked very funny indeed without a nose, and could only speak in muffled croaks, tried to shout: 'Hussy! Are you too not going to die of shame?' But all Macha could do was burst out laughing. He took hold of his sword and went for her: 'Any woman who finds out how easily a man's nose comes off has learned the Secret of the Land and she must die!' And at that he lunged with his sword at her heart, but she was too quick. He fell over his tangled veils, which were all about his feet.

Macha ran out of the house and through the streets, shouting, *'Ní scéal rúin é ó tá a fhios ag triúr é!'*, which meant, 'it is not a secret if it is known to three people.' But all the doors and windows were shut and all the people put their fingers in their ears. There were still two more who needed to know the Secret. She ran faster and faster, like the wind, down the lanes, over the bogs, and deep into the forest where no-one had ventured ever before. There she found a little hut. She could barely make out the words to the humming noise that came from inside:

*'Pill a cake, roll a cake,*
*Budgeen and a thumb,*
*I'll bake you a cake*
*As quick as they come ...'*

She stood on the window-sill and peered in. There was an old woman inside: she wore no veil. Even though Macha coughed and tapped at the pane, the old woman was too busy kneading dough, pulling it and rolling it, to notice. She was red in the face with her work, putting pieces of rolled dough into the oven and taking other pieces out. What Macha saw so astonished her that she fell right in through the window. There were noses, hundreds and thousands of noses, all different sizes and shapes. The old woman would take a bit of paper out of her pocket, examine it, check the list against the number of noses in front of her, sometimes fly into a temper, hurl some noses to the floor, stamp on them, and put the dough back in to the basin and begin the kneading all over again.

Macha's heart began to beat very fast. She forgot her manners and burst out, 'Who told you the Secret? And who told you to make the noses?' The old woman spun around, roaring with laughter, whirling faster and faster until Macha thought she would disappear altogether. 'Bless me, bless me, the ignorance of this young one! We don't call them noses, we call them budgeens. Men cannot live unless they have their budgeens. I make all the budgeens, I am the *budgeen-maker*.'

Macha faced her: and for the first time in her life she felt fear. 'Why do you keep it a secret and frighten us all?' At this, the old woman stopped her spinning, came firmly down upon her two feet, fixed Macha with eyes like steel. She barked: 'I keep nothing secret! You are keeping a secret from me. Tell it!' Macha said, 'I can't tell it. Because *ní scéal rúin é ó tá a fhios ag triúr é.*' The old woman pursed her lips with annoyance: '*Is olc an chearc nach scríobann di féin:* it's a bad hen that does not scratch for herself! I've been too busy, keeping the breath inside men, to scratch around and know what's going on behind my back! That robber of a king, that gombeen, that grabber, not letting the women know

Kate White

that men's budgeens fall off! And that I am the one who puts them back on! So that's his power! He sells my new budgeens and tells the men that *he* makes them, gripping all the praise for himself, and keeping it a secret too! No more, no more. He can fool some of the people all of the time and all of the people some of the time but he won't fool old Morrígan more than once! I'm going on strike, I'm retiring. Let *you* take your turn at keeping the world going.'

And thereupon she blew out her fire, dismantled her oven, put it in her pocket, poured water on all the dough, and threw it out of the hut so ferociously that all the animals, birds and plants of the forest began to screech in chorus, 'Tell it to a third,' they screamed, 'tell it to a third, Macha, tell it to a third!' Old Morrígan got hold of her bellows and began puffing the air between Macha's feet so vigorously that the girl lost her balance and floated up into the air, out of the window, and over the trees. As she went, she heard Morrígan's voice like a thin pipe following her: 'You have already one gift, the gift of fearlessness: I give you two more - the gift of speed and the gift of the budgeen-recipe.'

Macha's veil was like a sail: it carried her over mountains, rivers, and lakes, like a white mare flying, then a grey one, then a black one. At nightfall she alighted at a small farm-house. Inside there was a man asleep. By his posture he seemed a very wretched unhappy man. She took the veil off his face and never had she seen such a miserable budgeen in all her life, it was all cracked and soggy.

She went to the cupboard, got a bowl, fresh flour and water, lit the oven; and in few minutes had baked him a fine brown shiny new one, and stroked it into place. The man (whose name was Crunnchu) woke up dancing with joy. 'I'm a new man, I've no need to go to the king anymore, I have *you*! Are we not the best match?' 'We are,' she said, 'but never tell the king!'

So for a while they lived happily together, until one day a message came from the king that there was a great curse upon the land and all the men had to come to his council. Crunnchu went. Late that night he returned and said, 'Oh, what have I done? I've let the cat out of the bag. The king told us the land is cursed because there are no new noses: and I was fool enough to tell him that you, Macha, are a budgeen-maker and could lift the curse. The king said, "Bring her to me": and I knew from the way he winked that once he has your recipe from you he will kill you.' Macha smiled to herself, because she still had one gift the king knew nothing of. 'Go back to the king, and tell him I will be glad to meet him: on one condition. It must be tomorrow, the day of the horse-races, and the king's horse must race against me.' Crunnchu implored her not to be so reckless. How could a woman run faster than a horse? She repeated her command, and he did her bidding.

The king thought it a great joke. But Macha stayed up all night, baking.

The next day she arrived at the assembly with a bag of new budgeens strapped to her back. The horn sounded, the race commenced. Her gift of speed from Morrígan brought her to the winning-post in one leap: she faced the king as he galloped toward her. She opened her mouth, and it grew, and grew, wider and wider. The wider her mouth grew, the more the men froze with fear. Then she swallowed the king, right out of his saddle.

She hitched up her skirts and began a jig, kicking her

legs higher and higher; the women threw off their veils, hitched up *their* skirts too, and *their* legs likewise were joining in the jig. All that could be seen were the legs up and down in the air and the noise was like a hundred thunderstorms; the birds joined in and the fishes from the sea, and all the creatures of the land, even the sun and the moon.

The women picked up the cry, 'Tell it to a third, tell it to a third!' As she danced, Macha gave a great gulp of breath, and out shot the king into the crowd from between her thighs. He fell to the ground in one place; and his budgeen fell in another, crumbling into dust.

She said, 'There's a new one for you in the sack on my back.' How the women laughed to see him crawl to put it on!

'If men steal women's work,' she said, 'and claim it for their own, I will not just swallow *one*, but the *lot* of you!' And the men never dared pull such a stroke ever again.

*Margaretta D'Arcy*

# The Witch-Hunt

INSIDE HER small, sparsely-furnished cottage, Minnie Power was making preparations for her evening visitors. A turf fire burned brightly in the wide, open hearth. Leaping tongues of flames licked the bottom of a huge three-legged cauldron which hung from an iron crane in the fire's recess. Minnie's large, black cat, Psyche, relaxed contentedly in an armchair near the hob.

Darkness was closing in and the dancing light from the fire threw shadows and strange shapes on the walls and ceiling. In the centre of the room stood a long wooden table covered with bottles of every size, shape and hue; some full, some empty, and all labelled. Books on plants, herbs, spices, medicines and the anatomy of the human body occupied a large bookcase against one wall. Over all hung a delicate fragrance of herbs and spices.

As she busied herself stirring the cauldron with a longhandled enamel spoon and filling the bottles with her lotions and potions, Minnie crooned softly while Psyche purred loudly. Occasionally, she consulted a book which lay open on the table.

Minnie was reputed to be a witch. Her one and only companion was Psyche, who, people said, turned into a she-devil at night and was really Minnie's sister. Minnie herself did nothing to dispel these rumours, rather she reinforced them by her eccentric dress and, at times, odd behaviour.

Mystery surrounded her past. No one knew exactly where she had come from, so there was much speculation about her background. Some said she had been a wealthy woman who had suffered a sad misfortune and was now forced to live in reduced circumstances. Others said she was the daughter of a bishop who had her banished from his sight, or that she was an ex-nun, discharged for insubordinate behaviour. Nobody ever said 'hello' to Minnie. As she passed by, people would cross themselves and mutter, 'The Lord between us and all harm.'

Although publicly Minnie was ostracised, privately she was much sought after. Over the years she had earned a reputation for being able to cure certain ailments and was particularly wise in matters affecting women's health and well-being. At first, no one was ever seen paying her a visit but as her curative powers became better known more and more women called for advice. It was at this juncture that Minnie's problems really began.

The first client to arrive, on this particular day, was Julia Mac who was married to Johnny, the blacksmith. She looked hot and flustered so Minnie offered her a cup of camomile tea.

'Take it easy, Julia. You know what I told you about the blood pressure. Sit down and relax.'

'Thanks, Minnie, the drop of tea is very welcome but I haven't come about myself. It's about you. I felt I had to warn you. You've been so good to me in the past. You're the talk of the town and your name was read from the pulpit on Sunday. Holy God, but it's a fright, so it is.'

It was probably only a coincidence, but at the mention of the deity, Psyche stretched her legs and bared her claws. Minnie lifted her off the chair and sat down with her in her lap. She whispered a soothing word in her ear.

'I'm used to talk, Julia. You have to develop a thick skin in my line of business. Anyway, when they are talking about me they are leaving others alone.'

But that's where you are wrong,' said Julia, shaking her head. 'It's not just talk and they're not leaving others alone either. They're saying that you are performing fertility rites in the woods at night, getting couples to leap through blazing bonfires, and that you sent Peg Mannion to the city for an unmentionable operation. It's all the fault of the apothecaries and specialists who believe you are queering their pitch.They see you as a threat to their interests. And that's not the holy all of it either. Take a look at what was given out at the church last Sunday.'

Julia produced a leaflet and thrust it into Minnie's hands. As she read it her expression grew very sad.

### BEWARE! SATAN IS AT WORK!

*It has come to the notice of concerned citizens of this town that Satan is in our midst in the form of a WITCH. Certain unnatural practices are taking place in the home of Minnie Power which are a threat to our Christian society. All right-minded people are called upon to gather outside The Witch Power's Cottage at sundown on Wednesday.*
*Lend a hand in driving Satan from our town.*
*Organised by the CITIZENS UNITED against PAGAN SORCERY (CUPS)*

Julia could see that Minnie was very distressed. 'You'll have to leave, Minnie. It isn't safe for you to stay here any more.'

Kate White

For a moment Minnie said nothing. Then she stood up straight and tossed her head defiantly, crumpled the leaflet and threw it into the fire. It roared up the chimney in a ball of flame.

'I have no intentions of running away, Julia, because I have done nothing wrong. I will stand my ground and trust in the women whom I have helped over the years. They will explain how I listened to their problems, which the professionals wouldn't even admit existed, how I provided them with alternative medicines when others only patronised them, telling them to go home and pull themselves together or else doped them with drugs. They will tell how I comforted and counselled.'

'That high-minded talk is all very well, if you don't mind me saying so,' said Julia, 'but I've spoken to some of the women and not all of them are brave enough to stand up and be counted. Don't you see, they don't have your independent mind and attitude? You must go into hiding and when it's safe you can make your whereabouts known to us somehow. Don't let the CUPS get you - we need you, Minnie.'

'Thank you, Julia, for your kindness and solidarity but the time has now come to face the mindless mob. I have been hounded for too many years. Besides, you will be surprised at the support I will get.'

Julia was disappointed that Minnie wouldn't take her advice. 'I hope you won't regret it. The fanatics in CUPS will stop at nothing to achieve their ends, wait till you see. But you can count on me no matter what.'

On the evening of the demonstration, people began to arrive just before dusk carrying an effigy of Minnie hanging from a pole. They became rowdy, chanting 'We want the Witch,' and throwing stones at the windows. Then they made a huge circle and set fire to the effigy. All the while, Minnie sat at the fire stroking Psyche. Every time a window pane broke the cat let out a caterwaul, which excited the mob even more.

In the middle of the commotion the police arrived and through a loudhailer they ordered Minnie to come to the front door. When she did the crowd went wild. She was then formally charged with performing unlawful acts of witchcraft and with being the cause of a riot. She was marched off to the market place where she was clamped in the pillory for the night. At the inquisition to be held next day, she would be further charged with bewitching the women of the town, dealing in incantations, charms and spells, encouraging women to visit other witches in the city, concocting love potions and telling fortunes.

Meanwhile, Psyche had made good her escape and was down in the woods frightened out of her wits. Her pitiful screams were soon heard by the local fairy group who emerged from their rath to investigate. Fairies and animals have no difficulty in communicating with each other, so in no time at all the fairies had the whole story.

Some of the more undisciplined fairies suggested a blast from the Evil Eye was the only way to break the CUPS and lessen their power, but they were overruled and it was finally decided to rescue Minnie from the pillory and take her into safe keeping. Psyche, who was very streetwise, led a procession into the town while the humans slept. When they reached the pillory poor Minnie was unconscious and looked very much the worse for her experience. She was so well secured with huge iron locks that, try as they would, they were unable to free her.

Then Psyche had an idea. 'I'll go for Johnny the Blacksmith, who is married to Julia Mac. He will pick the locks without any bother and Julia will be a comfort to Minnie.'

The head fairy thought this was a great idea. 'We will bestow on you the magic power to turn yourself into a human when you reach the forge because Johnny would have a heart attack if he heard a cat talk.'

When Johnny heard the rescue plan he gathered some tools while Julia yoked the horse and cart. In no time at all they were back at the pillory where Minnie was being kept warm by the fairies and quicker than you could say, 'Women of the World Unite, You've nothing to lose but your Pillories,' Minnie was free.

Minnie has been underground ever since but with the help of Psyche and the fairies she is continuing to keep in contact with the women of the town. Her work carries a great deal of danger because the CUPS are still determined to discredit her and banish her for ever.

*Máirín Johnston*

# Snow-Fight Defeats Patri Arky

SNOW-FIGHT lived with her cousins the Arky family. She had been living there since her mother had died many years before. Though she had been called Snow-White at birth she preferred the name Snow-Fight, which her cousin Patri had begun to call her soon after her arrival, due to their constant arguments about sharing housework.

Snow-Fight had large green eyes and curly red hair, and her skin was so fair that her nine freckles looked as if they had been painted on. She had tried to get along with her cousins, but every day seemed to bring more disagreement and unhappiness.

'Where's my clean shirt?' Patri Arky asked, as he impatiently pulled all the neatly-folded clothes out of the hot press.

'When did you wash it?' retorted Snow-Fight.

'I!' exclaimed Patri. 'When did *I* wash it? Since when did a hard-working man like myself find time to do silly washing?'

'Well,' said Snow-Fight, 'clean shirts don't just appear, you know.'

'Hummph,' muttered Patri, 'I didn't ask for a treatise on the subject. I only want what is due to me.'

'Due? Due?' repeated Snow-Fight incredulously, 'No-one is *due* a clean shirt. You know where the washing machine and the iron are kept if it's a clean shirt you want.'

And so went another prelude to an argument in the Arky household on the politics of housework.

There were seven Arkys, five brothers and two sisters. Ann Arky had left home years before; she could not bear the way her brothers wanted everything organised to suit themselves, expecting herself and her older sister Matri to do simply everything around the house.

The eldest Arky was Olig. He was haughty and selfish. He insisted on taking the seat at the top of the table at meal times, the seat which was nearest the stove, caring only about his own warmth and comfort. He demanded his dinner first, and if he didn't get it, would sulk and make the meal miserable for everyone else.

Sometimes he had to shove Hier out of his place. Hier Arky was not quite as strong as Olig, but he admired the way his big brother got what he wanted all the time. He too bullied Matri as much as he could, and insisted on having his bed made and his potatoes mashed for him.

Next in age were the twins Mon and Noh Arky. Though twins, they were not alike: Mon (or Monty as he liked to be called) was fascinated by anything regal and he spent his days dreaming about ermine coats, thrones and palaces. He tried to order others around as if he were some kind of king!

Noh was a lovely lad, black-haired and gentle. He disliked fighting and never argued with his brothers, but he wished he was old enough to go off on an adventure, just like his big sister Ann.

Of all the boys, the one who disliked Snow-Fight most of all was Patri. He had been happy until she had

133

Kate White

turned up and though he had tried to turn Matri against Snow-Fight and stop her listening to the crazy notions of her cousin, he had failed. Patri had tried to bully Snow-Fight when she first arrived but with her red-haired temper and quick tongue he was no match for her. The only one Snow-Fight felt close to was Matri; she was quiet but strong and always intervened if the boys were giving Snow-Fight a hard time, which was often the case. They had become good friends and had great fun together, spending hours talking. Their favourite activity was going on picnics. They loved to walk from the Arky house deep into the woods, where they had discovered a path that led down to the sea-shore. Collecting shells and feathers was a shared passion. They were amazed at the colours and shapes of the shells and they tickled each other with silky feathers. It was always a treat to go out together.

Snow-Fight noticed how Matri was working increasingly hard in the house.

'I worry that you'll exhaust yourself, Matri', said Snow-Fight one day as they strolled along through the woods watching the squirrels collect walnuts.

'Oh Snow,' replied Matri, 'You are always worrying about me. Don't fret yourself.'

Snow-Fight nodded slowly, wishing that Matri had fewer demands on her time and didn't have to be constantly reminding her brother of basic things which Snow-Fight felt everyone should know.

None of the boys picked up their dirty clothes. The younger ones had learned the habits of the older boys, Olig and Patri, who were so jealous of Snow-Fight that they did things on purpose just to annoy her. Like the way they never put down the toilet seat before leaving the bathroom or they never had time to do the washing. The one occasion Olig did, he put everything in at once and shrank all the clothes.

Since their cousin had come to live with them, Matri was spending more time in the woods and at the sea than she did in the house. Oftentimes of late the boys had come home to find that their dinner was not ready. Things got even worse for the Arky boys. A dreadful thing occurred one Friday night; they arrived home to find a note on the fridge which said, 'Gone to an assertiveness training class', signed Matri.

Several weeks later Matri announced that Snow-Fight and herself were going to a dance and that none of the boys could go, as it was for women and girls only. This was the last straw. Patri decided that something would have to be done.

He thought up a clever plan, one which would ensure that Matri would stay in the house and which would also take care of that trouble maker Snow-Fight.

Late on the night of the dance Snow-Fight and Matri arrived home. They were laughing and singing songs about women's armies and becoming engineers. Patri was about to tell them to be quiet when he heard other singing voices. With Snow-Fight and Matri were the three Fury sisters. They were bright energetic young women, and had been the organizers of the dance. The five women were swearing loudly that they would all organize another such evening very soon. As they left they sang 'I will Survive' in harmony.

Above them in his dark bedroom Patri heard this, and he vowed that if the house was going to be filled with cackling women in this manner on a regular basis, the sooner he carried out his plan the better.

Next day, Snow-Fight woke early and went out to the woods for her morning jog. She did her warm-ups and set off down the worn path towards the sea. There by a large oak was an old man, with a basket of ripe red apples.

'Have a pretty apple, my dear,' said the crackly voice.

'Apples! - you've got to be joking!' puffed Snow-Fight. 'They're either pumped full of chemicals or else irradiated to make them stay fresh. No, thanks.' She called back over her shoulder, 'I haven't eaten apples for years.' And she jogged off down the path to the strand.

The disguised Patri sat bewildered; his clever plan had not worked. He *had* to get Snow-Fight somehow. None of the old tricks would work on her. He decided to enlist the help of his old school buddies, the Crats.

The Crats lived two miles away and Patri remembered how they had always been such allies at school. He knew he could depend on their help when they heard how Snow-Fight was disrupting the household.

Otto Crat and Techno Crat listened carefully to Patri. Otto never allowed anyone inside his house, so Patri was given a lecture on how to remain boss in your own home. It was not to Otto Crat that Patri applied for practical assistance, but to Techno.

Techno Crat brought Patri into his laboratory and here Patri saw all sorts of wonders that Techno was developing. There were gigantic rats and miniscule elephants and little puppies with no tails.

'These', laughed Techno, 'are my pets, they help me greatly with my work, as you can see,' and he pointed to rows of cages which lined the walls of his laboratory.

Patri smiled nervously and reminded Techno of his problem. From a long line of test-tubes Techno chose a white liquid which he poured into a tiny phial.

'Put this into her tea and she won't make a sound for years,' snorted Techno. Patri laughed with him as he slipped the thin phial into his pocket and set off for home.

Snow-Fight didn't drink tea or coffee but Patri knew how much she loved a glass of soya milk before her jog. So when he got home and no-one was looking he emptied the contents of the phial into her soya milk flask. He didn't have long to wait. That evening as Noh and Mon were walking through the woods they found Snow-Fight stretched out on the path. Tearfully they carried her home and with Olig's help they laid her on the bed. Her face was cold as ice and her breath was barely there, yet Matri saw that she was asleep. It puzzled her to know how Snow-Fight, her beautiful friend, had collapsed into this deep sleep.

Patri hugged himself with glee, thrilled that Snow-Fight was at last silent and that Matri would now be obliged to stay put. He had sorted it all out!

'Soon things will be back to the way they were before Snow-Fight arrived,' he whispered to himself as he settled down for the night.

For three days his plan worked beautifully. Matri threw herself into the housework, stopping only to check on Snow-Fight. But there was no change in her condition. She slept silently, growing paler each day. On the fourth day there was a loud knock and into the kitchen stumbled the three Fury sisters.

'Oh, Matri, how awful, we've just heard about Snow-Fight,' and the three women put their arms around Matri as she burst into tears and wept.

In no time the three Furys had organized things. They took turns sitting with Snow-Fight and they

138

stroked her and spoke to her, even sang, in an effort to waken her. By the time Patri got home his plan had fallen apart. The Furys had decided they would move in and devote their time to Snow-Fight. Matri was, of course, glad of their offer and loved their company. Soon the house was full of their singing and humming. They only visited the kitchen to make soup for Matri or herbal tea for themselves. There were grumblings from the younger Arky boys but when they realised that no cooking or housework would be done while Snow-Fight was ill, they got stuck in themselves. All, that is, except Patri Arky. He sat slumped on the sofa listening to the crooning and cackling of the women.

'I can't stand this,' he said as he buried his face in his hands; though he hated to admit defeat he knew that events had taken such a turn against him that things would never be the same again. So he packed a bag and as the clock struck eleven he slipped out of the little house on the edge of the woods and decided to go to find a place where he would receive the respect and attention that he was due.

'Somewhere that those horrid ideas of Snow-Fight's haven't been heard of,' he thought hopefully. 'Ah, for the good old days,' he sighed, as he put distance between himself and the little house.

Patri Arky could not have been gone more than an hour when the front door flew open and in marched Ann Arky, a tall woman with long chestnut-coloured hair and a broad smile on her face. She bounded up the stairs to Snow-Fight's room and the women within shrieked with joy at the sight of their long-lost sister and friend.

Ann Arky had had such adventures. She was now a world-famous scientist and had discovered excellent things like cures for diseases and natural remedies that had long been forgotten. None of her knowledge came from harming animals; she had collected the wisdom of all the wise healers she had met on her travels and she knew just what Snow-Fight needed.

From beneath her purple shawl she pulled a small glass bottle. In it was a mixture of herbs and mosses. She instructed the other women as she placed a drop of this potion on Snow-Fight's eyes and lips. Each of the women kissed Snow-Fight in turn and they all held hands and sang an ancient rhyme which Ann Arky taught them.

> *Women are we, sisters are we,*
> *We have the power to heal ourselves,*
> *We kill no beasts, we poison no lands,*
> *The power is ours, it is in our hands.*

As the last note was sung a sweet perfume filled the room, Snow-Fight opened her eyes and the women laughed and cheered with relief and happiness.

By the next morning the six women had decided that they would live together, with and for each other. The boys Olig, Mon, Hier and Noh finally agreed that they would build a house further into the wood and that they would visit their sisters and cousin. Before they left each of them promised that they would never expect any woman to clean and cook for them. In fact, Noh and Mon were signing up for the Cordon Bleu cookery class in the local school next term. Snow-Fight believed that now Patri Arky was gone the boys would indeed try to keep their promise.

None of these women thought that they would live happily ever after, as the story goes, but they knew that they would live equally, and what could be nicer?

*Gráinne Healy*

# Thumbelina, the Left Wing Fairy

Once upon a time in the Land of Nod lived a tiny girl called Thumbelina. No one shook hands or said 'hello' in this land. Instead everyone nodded and winked all the time because a nod was as good as a wink, although nods were used for strangers and winks for people you knew well and liked.

People slept a lot of the time in the Land of Nod because no one wanted to make a sound. People who lived by the sea didn't want to rock the boat because that would make waves. You could hear a pin drop any hour of the day and when it did everyone scurrried in fear of the giant. To these little thumbsize creatures when the penny dropped it sounded as if someone had dropped a clanger. It dropped once a year when the giant was counting his money. He had so much piled on his table he couldn't budge it. It glistened and gleamed but the giant couldn't count it because he had sticky fingers. With the money that stuck to his fingers he played push ha'penny with himself. But this giant was very stupid. He didn't know that one and one makes two so, since he made the rules, he decided that the first goal scored won the game. He spent a lot of time tabling motions until he finally scored. That was when the penny slid off the table and dropped into the grass.

Down in the grass roots lived the little people. The

Paula Nolan

giant was big and strong and lived very far removed from the grass roots. His name was Jargon but his friends called him Cliche. He got where he was by having a party and walking all over everyone. Every year the balloons in his party caused inflation and the little people were fed up with all the hot air. Nevertheless they ran to the tree and waited for the crumbs from the rich man's table. When the penny dropped they turned it into a table and sat around the table and made laws. These were called the tables of the law. To finish annual general meetings everyone cried 'Holy Moses', but no one knew why.

Little Thumbelina slept most of her life. The penny dropped when she was born. People used to give her the thumbs-up on rare occasions when she left her bed and the rest of the time they talked about her as a gifted dreamer. Then one day she woke up.

She climbed the tree to the top until she held the floor. Then she took the chair and climbed and climbed until she tabled a motion and found herself at the top of the heap. The giant stirred in his sleep. The money was all piled up on the right. She pushed the money to the left until it came raining down into the grass roots and all the little people woke up. Now everyone had a table and each individual could make their own laws to suit themselves.

Ever since then people in the Land of Nod have lived by rule of thumb and no-one has been any the wiser.

*Joni Crone*